PRAISE FOR *BARBARA THE SLUT AND OTHER PEOPLE*

Named a "Best Book of the Year" by *Publishers Weekly*

"There isn't a bad part of *Barbara the Slut*. . . . The stories in this book are sometimes painful, sometimes brilliantly funny, and most often both; Holmes can find the humor in the worst situations, and the tragedy in the most glorious moments. But it's her characters who carry the stories—imperfect, difficult, and defiantly human." —NPR

"Like the best work of Mary Gaitskill, *Barbara the Slut* turns our obsession with sex on its head in order to study it, dissect it, weaponize it. Case in point: the promiscuous high school student who finds the word 'slut' painted on her locker. Where other young women might buckle at the slur, she likes the color of paint the vandals used. She refuses to be shamed, and her refusal is empowering, rare, and, well, pretty sexy."

—*Esquire*

"Holmes trains a precise lens on the millennial generation's mixed bag of manners, mores, and machinations. . . . In [these] beautifully brazen stories, worlds collide in fresh, imaginative ways." —*Elle*

"Holmes brings a cool, stripped-down wit to [these] ten shaggy-dog stories . . . loopy, deadpan, and accidentally-on-purpose profound."

—*Entertainment Weekly*

"Living can be a distressingly solitary activity and Holmes . . . explores this hard truth with unexpected poignancy, subtlety and humor. . . . [She] could write from the point of view of a Tupperware bowl and it would be compelling." —*Chicago Tribune*

"In a time when most women don't truly own the word 'slut,' much less claim it, the book is a rallying cry." —*The Washington Post*

"With the polished prose and a wry dash of Miranda July–esque humor, Holmes has created a normcore cast of characters who stumble to communicate, withhold their true identities, and soldier through the slow letdowns of life. . . . Like a shot of espresso, these tales awaken the senses and invigorate the daily grind." —*O, The Oprah Magazine*

BARBARA THE SLUT

and Other People

Lauren Holmes

Riverhead Books / New York

For my family

RIVERHEAD BOOKS
An imprint of Penguin Random House LLC
375 Hudson Street
New York, New York 10014

The Library of Congress has catalogued the Riverhead hardcover edition as follows:

Holmes, Lauren, date.
  [Short stories. Selections.]
  Barbara the slut and other people / Lauren Holmes.
      p.   cm.
  ISBN 9781594633782
  I. Title.
PS3608.O49435455A6   2016   2015004287
813'.6—dc23

First Riverhead hardcover edition: August 2015
First Riverhead trade paperback edition: August 2016
Riverhead trade paperback ISBN: 9780399576034

Printed in the United States of America
10   9   8   7   6   5   4   3   2

Book design by Meighan Cavanaugh

CONTENTS

HOW AM I SUPPOSED
TO TALK TO YOU?

In Mexico City the customs light lit up green, which was lucky because I had fifty pairs of underwear with tags on them in my suitcase. They were from Victoria's Secret and they were for my mom to sell to the teenagers in her town for a markup of three hundred percent. She managed a hotel in Pie de la Cuesta, a fishing town six miles west of Acapulco, and she said the kids there wanted this underwear more than marijuana. I thought this sounded like a second grader's plan, but I said I would do it because I hadn't visited her in three years.

In addition to bringing my mom the underwear, I was supposed to use this trip to tell her I was gay, to ask her to start talking to Grandpa again so I didn't have to feel bad about taking his tuition checks, and to generally make up for the ten years I was in California, in middle school and high school and college, and she was in Mexico, in the city and then at the beach.

She was supposed to meet me at the airport, but at the last minute she told me it was safer to take buses than cars late at night. She said I had taken buses in Mexico before but I was pretty sure I hadn't. All the other times I'd visited my mom in Mexico, she'd been living at her parents' house in Mexico City, and Grandpa's driver would come and get me at the airport.

My mom told me to take a taxi from the airport to the south bus station, a bus from there to Acapulco, and another bus from Acapulco to Pie de la Cuesta. In Mexico City, the taxi passed the exit for Río Piedad, and I wished I were going to Grandpa's house. My mom had told me not to tell him I was coming, but now I wondered if it would be a good way to get her to talk to him, to tell her she had to come to his house if she wanted to see me. In the meantime I could go to sleep right away, and swim in Grandpa's pool, and have his driver go get me tacos.

I slept on the bus to Acapulco, and when we got there it was still dark. I was half awake waiting for the bus to Pie de la Cuesta and when it came it wasn't a bus with air-conditioning and a stewardess and soda and chips like the one I'd just taken. It was a city bus that wound along the coast at what felt like a hundred miles an hour, but when the bus wasn't turning and I wasn't looking off the dark cliff, I realized it was probably more like twenty. The five other passengers were asleep. Only the bus driver and I were awake and listening to the staticky radio.

The sun rose behind the bus. I started to get nervous when we wound down the cliff. My mom said that when the bus got to town and passed her pink hotel, El Flamenco, I was supposed to yell *"¡Bajan!"* and get out. As we drove, there were more and more houses on the right side of the road and more and more hotels on the left side, where the beach was. Finally the houses were stuck together, and the hotels were almost stuck together. The hotels looked like motels to me, and there was more than one pink one. Finally I saw El Flamenco and stood up to yell but I couldn't do it. I sat back down and pretended like, *Oh man, I almost got off at the wrong stop again.* Five hotels and ten houses later, the teenager in the backseat yelled, *"¡Bajan!"* and I got off with him. I pulled out the handle of my suitcase and started walking back toward the motel.

My mom was standing outside, under a string of lights. "Lala!" she said and ran toward me. She was wearing woven shorts and a white tank top and she looked really good. Her boobs were huge and her arms were toned and she was so brown.

She gave me a million kisses all over my face and my hands. She touched my hair, which had always been long but now was short. She started to cry.

"Hi Mama," I said.

"Hi baby," she said. "I knew that was your bus. You're so beautiful." She took my free hand and I wheeled my suitcase into the courtyard. There was a pool in the middle with strings of lights around it, and the doors to the rooms were around the courtyard in an L shape. The office was separate from the L, between the pool and the street.

She opened the door and we went inside. It was cool in there and I wondered if she was the only person in Pie de la Cuesta with air-conditioning. Her apartment was above the office, and we walked up the stairs. It looked like no one lived there—there were no plants or pictures or glasses of water, just a couch and a wooden chair in the living room, and a square table and two more chairs in the kitchen. In the bedroom she put my suitcase down. There was a bed with no frame and another chair. But the bed had her same white sheets on it, these sheets that cost a million dollars and feel like clouds and smell like clouds.

My mom got into the bed and I got in with her. She traced the spot on my forehead where she said I had a swirl of hair as a baby. Every muscle in my body relaxed. She stroked my head and then I was ten years old and we were lying in the cloud sheets in Los Angeles and I was crying because we had to put our dog Maria von Trapp to sleep. That night my mom had stroked my head until I fell asleep. I don't know where my dad was—he was there when we put Maria to sleep but then not there later.

After a while my mom said, "Are you hungry, baby?" and it brought me back to the present and being twenty and I felt embarrassed to be in bed with my mom. I wanted to sit up but I was too weak. I tried to open my eyes and my mom laughed at me.

"I'm starving," I said.

She went to the kitchen and made me an egg sandwich, which is one of my favorite things, with Oaxacan cheese, which is another one of my favorite things. She cut up a papaya and two bananas and she ate the fruit while I ate the sandwich.

After breakfast I asked my mom if I could make a phone call.

"Of course, baby, who do you want to call?"

"I want to tell Dad I got in safe."

"Oh," she said. She said that the phone in the office didn't make long distance calls, but she gave me a phone card and told me there was a pay phone to the left of the hotel.

When I got to the phone I dialed Dana's number. I had told her I would call her every day but now that I was here I didn't really feel like it.

"Hey it's me," I said when she picked up.

"Hi!" she said. "I was so worried about you."

"Why?" I said. "I told you I would call you when I got here."

"I know, but I was worried. How's your mom?"

"She's fine. How are you?"

"I'm really great. I haven't eaten or used an animal product in forty-two days."

"Oh right," I said. "That's good."

"Did you come out to your mom yet?"

"No. I've only been here for like an hour."

"I can't wait for you to tell her. I'm so proud of you."

I told her I would call her the next day and then I hung up by accident.

Then I called my dad and made the mistake of telling him about the buses.

"You got in in the middle of the night," he said, "and your mother couldn't pick you up?"

"It's safer to take the buses at night," I said.

"This is not what we agreed," he said. "I'm going to call her."

"Dad. Please don't call her. I'm fine. I want to have a good time."

He said he would wait until I was back to call her, and I said okay and hoped he would forget by then. He told me to call Dana because she had called the house twice. He made me promise to wear sunscreen and to not go swimming. He said he was reading about Pie de la Cuesta on the internet and the undertow was deadly.

When I got back to the apartment my mom said, "Ready to go to the beach?"

"Yeah," I said.

"Do you have the underwear?" she said.

"Yeah." I opened my suitcase and took out the underwear and my bathing suit.

"Did you get the bags?" said my mom.

I was supposed to get fifty striped bags to go with the fifty pairs of underwear.

"They would only give me ten," I said and gave them to her.

"Okay," said my mom. "I can give them to the girls who buy a lot."

I went into the bathroom and took off my shorts and T-shirt. My mom came in behind me and snapped my underwear band and said, "You should get yourself some new underwear."

I imagined myself wearing the pair I had bought that said "Boys Boys Boys" a thousand times in black letters. My mom had said to get as many pairs with English words on them as possible. Another pair said "See you tonight," and I thought those were really funny, because if someone else was seeing them, wasn't it already tonight? Unless it was a reminder to yourself, like, see you tonight when I take my pants off again.

"I like my underwear," I said.

"They're kind of sturdy," said my mom. They were gray and boy-style but for girls, and I wondered if she thought they were butch. I wanted her to think so, so that I wouldn't have to tell her.

"I'm going to put my suit on, okay?" I said.

"Oh, okay," she said and left the bathroom.

When I was done I went back out to the living room. My mom came out of the bedroom wearing a terry cloth dress. "Do you want to borrow a beach dress?" she said.

"No," I said.

"We have to sell ourselves if we want to sell the underwear," she said.

"I don't want to sell myself," I said.

"Okay, don't sell yourself," said my mom, "sell the American dream."

"Really?" I said. "This underwear is going to fly people to the U.S. and get them green cards and jobs at hotels and then they're going to win the lottery?"

"Ha," said my mom. "Come on, let's go. I have to be back for checkout at noon."

"And then they'll buy forty cars and go bankrupt and have to come back to Mexico?"

"Ha ha. Are you ready?" She had the underwear sorted by size in three of the bags.

"We're selling the underwear now?" I said.

"Of course," she said. "It's Saturday, a lot of kids are going to be at the beach."

It was starting to get really hot outside. We walked through the row of palm trees that separated the hotels from the beach. On the other side was sand and water, and some sets of tables and chairs under a thatched roof. The sky was almost clear except for thin stripes of clouds. As we made our way to the water I saw that there were already people weaving in and out of the sunbathers and selling things—women with buckets of something, a woman carrying a bottle and calling *"Masajes, masajes,"* and a man leading a pony and offering rides. I wondered what my mom's plan was. She was ahead of me at the water.

"Put your feet in," she said. "It's nice."

I went in up to my knees and it was nice. The rest of my body was getting hot and I wanted to go in all the way. There were kids swimming and I wondered if my dad was wrong.

"I can go swimming, right?" I said.

"I wouldn't, baby, the current is so strong."

"Those kids are swimming."

"They're pros."

"I really want to go swimming," I said.

"You can swim in the pool," she said. "And I'll take you to the lagoon on Monday, it's gorgeous."

We walked along the water toward where it looked more crowded.

"So, are there any boys I should know about?" said my mom. Always her first question.

"Nope," I said. "Still no boys." That was always my answer, and she never seemed to think it was weird or some kind of clue, which she shouldn't have needed anyway. Shouldn't she have noticed when I was born? Wasn't there something about me that told her I was going to grow up to cut my hair and wear sturdy underwear and date a girl who brought her leather biker boots to textile recycling and then bought vegan ones? And if not when I was born, she should have noticed in elementary school when I was obsessed with amphibians and reptiles and with my friend Emily. And if still not then, she definitely would have noticed in middle school, when I hit puberty and was really confused and, according to my dad, really weird. But she was already gone.

I followed my mom out of the water and into the crowd of towels and people. She didn't say anything or approach anyone.

"How do you say 'underwear' again?" I said.

"*Pantis,*" said my mom.

"*¡Pantis! ¡Pantis!*" I called.

"Lala!" said my mom.

"What?"

"I was going to go up to girls that looked like they would want them."

"Okay," I said, "good plan."

We walked through the people until my mom spotted four girls and an older man together. She went up to them and said she was selling *ropa interior* from Victoria's Secret, and would they like to buy any.

One girl sat straight up and said, "*¡Papá, me encanta Victoria's Secret!*"

The dad looked at her and at my mom and frowned. "Huh," he said.

The other girls sat up too, and soon my mom was spreading out the underwear on one of their towels. The daughter picked out like eight pairs. One of the other girls looked at "See you tonight" and said, "Hubba hubba."

"Those are my favorite," I said.

"*Su favorito,*" said my mom.

I wasn't sure that they were impressed with me because I was starting to get really sweaty, but the daughter grabbed a pair of the same ones and looked at her dad.

"*¿A cuanto?*" he asked my mom.

"*Ciento cincuenta.*"

The dad raised his eyebrows but they bought three pairs. Then we sold some more pairs to another group of girls nearby, and when we were walking away my mom said, "See?"

. . .

Back at the motel my mom checked some Swiss people out and I went swimming in the pool. Later my mom came out and read, and I spent the afternoon sleeping until I was too hot, and then swimming until I was too tired.

At the end of the day we went back to the beach to watch the sunset. My mom said that when the sun set in Pie de la Cuesta, it lit up the backs of the waves, and you could see the silhouettes of kids swimming. Tonight the waves were too small, although they didn't look small to me. If I were braver I would have gone in and felt the water rush over my body and my head, and I probably would have been fine. But I was scared. My mom wasn't one to tell me something was dangerous if it wasn't. And she was sometimes one to tell me something was safe when it wasn't.

When the sun went down we went back to the apartment and got ready to go out to dinner. My mom came out of the bathroom with makeup on and said, "My friend is going to meet us at the restaurant. Is that okay?"

"A man?" I said.

"No, a woman. Of course, baby, a man. His name is Martin and he's from *Pah-ree*. You're going to love his accent." I assumed *Pah-ree* meant Paris.

"Great," I said.

The restaurant was ten motels down and when we got close we saw Martin waiting outside. He was tall and skinny and he waved at us.

"Oh shit, I forgot to tell you something," said my mom. "I only speak Spanish, okay? I'll explain later."

"How am I supposed to talk to you?" I said.

"You speak Spanish."

"I haven't spoken Spanish since I was five," I said.

Now Martin was twenty feet from us and he said, *"¡Hola!"*

"Bonsoir!" called my mom.

"Jesus," I said.

Martin gave my mom a kiss on the cheek. He shook my hand and gave me a kiss on the cheek too. He had a big nose but he was handsome and he had a lot of hair, which my mom likes. He didn't have a French mustache or anything. He was wearing a white button-up shirt and gray shorts.

The restaurant was a big patio, and there were folding chairs and folding tables with picnic covers. There were a lot of families with little kids. We sat at a table in the back and it felt like we were right on the beach. It was dark but I could see the waves licking the sand.

I ordered a piña colada and my mom ordered a bottle of wine for her and Martin.

I looked at the menu and didn't know what any of the

fish were except for *camarones*, and I hate shrimp. "I don't know what to get," I said in English.

"The *pulpo*, it is very good," said Martin. "This is octopus."

"A ella no le gusta comer pulpo," said my mom. *"Mija, te encantaría el pargo de piedra."*

"Okay," I said.

While we were waiting for our food, Martin asked me what I was studying in school. I gave him the speech I give strangers about my research—how there's so much information about lead poisoning in paint, but almost none about lead in soil, and kids are so much more likely to eat soil, and the community where I'm doing research relies on its gardens for food.

"This is very interesting," said Martin. "Your mother has not told me about this."

"Te lo he dicho," said my mom. *"Pero es tan complicado y ella es tan inteligente."*

They talked to each other in Spanish for the rest of the dinner, about me and stuff that I did when I was a kid, like one time in San Francisco when I kept catching fish and no one else caught any and they thought I could talk to animals. My mom said she knew I was going to be a doctor or a scientist. I tried to laugh at the right times but I had trouble following what they were saying.

After dinner we said good-bye to Martin and he walked in the other direction. On the way back to the motel, my mom told me that Martin didn't know about Grandpa or Grandma or that she had lived in the States with me and Dad. She thought he wouldn't think she was interesting if he knew that Grandpa was rich and not Mexican, and that Grandma came from a government family and was legally Mexican, but genetically at least fifty percent Spanish, and emotionally one hundred percent white. My mom didn't want Martin to know that she spoke English and went to Berkeley and lived in California for fourteen years and drove a Mercedes and then a Range Rover, so she told him she lived in Mexico City the whole time and drove her old VW the whole time, and I went to live with my dad in the States so I could go to a good school. My mom said the first time they met, Martin told her he loved her simple life, and she didn't want to tell him about me at all, but then she had to because I was coming.

When we got back to the apartment my mom kept her sandals on.

"Baby, you're just going to go to sleep, right? Would you mind if I went to Martin's apartment to say good night, and I'll come right back?"

"Sure," I said.

"Are you just going to go to sleep?"

"I think so," I said. "I'm exhausted."

"Okay baby, you go to bed then. Do you have everything you need?"

"Yeah."

My mom left and I took off my dress and put on a tank top. I washed my feet in the shower and brushed my teeth with her toothbrush. I got into bed with my book but when I put my head on the pillow it was all I could do to reach over and turn off the light before I fell asleep.

When I woke up it was early. The light coming into the room was white but not hot. I looked at the clock and it was seven twenty. I didn't want to wake up my mom so I read in bed until seven forty. Then I really had to pee, so I left the room quietly and was about to turn into the bathroom when I realized there was no one on the couch.

"Mom?" I said.

She wasn't in the bathroom and she wasn't in the kitchen, and I figured she must be in the office doing an early checkout or something. I peed and put on shorts and a T-shirt and went downstairs, hoping that no one would see me.

She wasn't in the office and she wasn't outside the office and I didn't see her going in or out of any of the guest rooms. I went back up to the apartment. I had a feeling she was still at Martin's, but what if she wasn't? I started to feel sick. I sat down in one of the chairs in the kitchen. What if something happened to her when she was walking back from Martin's? There was this town in Maine where I went with my dad and his girlfriend a couple of summers in high school, and every year when we got there, there had just been a murder on the beach. The murders were never premeditated; they just happened because drunk people got knives, or people with knives got drunk.

I was sure my mom was fine but my chest felt tight. I picked up my book to distract myself but I couldn't read. I felt like I should eat something but I wasn't hungry. Finally I did the kind of breathing my doctor taught me to help me sleep at night, where you breathe in and breathe out and you don't think about anything else, which I now know is called meditation. It never worked that well for me but I didn't know what else to do. I thought I should call Martin, but I didn't have his number or know where he lived.

Instead I called Dana from the phone in the office. I hoped it cost a million dollars.

"Hello?" said Dana. "Lala!" I had woken her up. "Did you do it?"

"What?"

"Did you tell her?"

"What? No. I don't even know where she is."

"What? What do you mean?"

"I don't know where she is. I think she's at her boyfriend's house. But she never came back last night."

"Oh my god, Lala, that's horrible."

"It's fine," I said. "I'm sure she'll be home any minute."

"God, I hope so," she said. "Are you going to tell her when she gets back?"

"Yes," I said. "Of course, I'll tell her right away."

"Are you being sarcastic?"

"Not at all," I said. "Maybe I'll hide in the kitchen and when she comes in I'll jump out and shout, 'I'm gay!'"

"You're being sarcastic."

I told Dana I had to go. Even when I found my mom, I wasn't going to tell her. Maybe I would tell Dana that I did it and that my mom and I both cried, and my mom told me she knew all along and she loved me no matter what. I didn't think it would count as lying because it didn't really matter if my mom knew or not.

I hung up and dialed my grandpa in Mexico City.

I heard the office door open a little after nine, and I heard my mom's sandals on the stairs. I went into the living room as she opened the door to the apartment.

"Baby," she said. "I didn't think you'd be up."

"Where were you?" I said. I didn't want to touch her but I gave her a hug because I wanted to feel that she was okay.

"I stayed at Martin's. I thought I would get back before you got up."

"I got up really early," I said. "I had no idea where you were."

"Oh baby," she said.

"I thought something bad happened to you on the way back last night," I said.

"I'm sorry," she said. "I'm really sorry. Let me make you something to eat."

She went into the kitchen and started cutting up fruit and I went into the bedroom and started packing my bag.

When I went back to the kitchen she said, "What do you want to do today, baby? Do you want to just lie on the beach? You're so pale."

"That's because I thought you got murdered," I said.

"Oh Lala, are you really that upset about it? I wouldn't have left you if I knew you would worry, but you're a big girl, I thought you'd be fine."

"I wasn't fine," I said. "I think I might go to Grandpa's."

"What? Why?"

"Then you can hang out with Martin as much as you want."

"I only saw him when you were sleeping, baby. I didn't think you would care."

"And at dinner. And you said you were coming right back."

"Okay," she said. "I won't see him again while you're here. I'll take you to Acapulco. We'll go to the beach and we'll go see the cliff divers."

"I told Grandpa I was coming."

"You called him?" She started to cry.

"I'm sorry," I said. "I was mad."

She cried and cried and I looked at the ceiling.

Finally I felt too bad and said, "Maybe we can go to Acapulco before I leave."

She looked up. "Yeah?"

"Sure," I said. "It's on the way."

She cried harder for a few seconds and then she slowed down and her breathing went back to normal and after a minute she stood up and went to the sink and splashed her face with water.

"Should we go now?" she said. "We might make it to see the divers at noon."

"Sure," I said.

"If we wear bathing suits we can go to the beach after. You can go in the water there."

"Okay."

"I should bring that Victoria's Secret underwear. Those beaches are full of rich Mexicans. I could charge a lot more. I could make a killing."

"Great," I said. I could tell that this had been the plan all along. "Grandpa would help you, you know."

"That is such a smart idea, Lala. I don't know why I never thought of that."

"Fine," I said, stung.

"I'm sorry," she said. "That was mean."

We put on our suits and got ready to go.

"Should I bring my bag?" I said.

"It's up to you," she said.

"I can always bring it back here," I said.

"Right," she said, and gave me a weak smile.

We took the bus to Acapulco, and when we got there we bought juices and walked up to the Quebrada. I wheeled my suitcase and my mom carried her bags of underwear. When we got to the entrance she bought tickets, and we went in and found a spot at the wall. We could already see the divers on top of the cliff, in the bright sun. Below them, the cliff went down at an angle, and it looked like when they dove they were going to hit the rock.

"Martin and I came to see them at night," she said. "They dive with torches, and we met some of those boys. Some of them are pretty cute."

"Oh yeah?" I said.

"Yeah," she said. "You're going to meet such a cute boy, you'll see. I didn't meet your dad until the end of college."

It felt like I was either going to tell my mom in the next minute, or my mouth was going to do it for me. My heart started to pound.

"I don't want to meet a boy," I said.

"Oh I know, baby, all you want to do is your research. But that will change."

"No, Mama, I want to meet girls. I like girls."

"Oh," she said. Her eyebrows went up. "Wow."

"Yeah."

"I had no idea," she said.

"Really?" I said. "You never wondered about it?"

"No," she said.

I waited for her to say something and then I decided to help her because I didn't want to be mad at her.

"Now you're supposed to say that you love me no matter what," I said.

"Oh, baby," she said, "of course I love you no matter what." She pulled me into her shoulder and held me tight. "Of course I love you no matter what."

After a minute she said, "Are you going to tell your dad?"

"He knows," I said.

"Oh really?" she said. "How did he take that news?"

"Fine," I said.

"Huh," she said.

"Why wouldn't he?" I said.

"I don't know, he can be so rigid."

"He's been really good," I said.

Now there were more divers on top of the cliff and they stood in a circle and put their arms around each other and their heads down.

"When did you tell him?"

"I don't know," I said. "High school."

"Oh my god. Lala. Why didn't you tell me?"

"I don't know," I said. "It didn't seem urgent."

"Why are you telling me now?" She sounded mad.

"I don't know," I said. "There's this girl and she thought I should tell you."

"You didn't want to tell me?"

"No, I did, I wanted you to know."

Now one of the boys was climbing down the cliff, and he stopped and stood. The people around us cheered, and he flew off the cliff, his back arched and his arms spread like eagle wings.

"I wish you told me when you told your dad."

"You weren't there," I said.

The diver entered the water with a high splash.

"You came to visit," she said.

"I don't know, Mom."

She looked away and I could hear her breathing. "Lala, you are breaking my heart," she said. She didn't look at me. "I'll meet you outside." She walked up the stairs and I stayed and watched the cliff. The boys prayed and dove forward and backward and did flips and double flips. Right after they jumped they were still in front of the sun for a split second, and then they rushed into the water. At the beginning I had been worried about them, but now it seemed less real, like they were on automatic or something, or like I was watching them from very far away. From very far away I watched them jump off the cliff one or two at a time, and finally three at a time.

My mom was waiting outside the entrance for me. We walked back down to the Zócalo without talking. When we got there she said, "I guess you have to get on that bus, huh? If you want to get to the city before dark."

"You could come to Grandpa's," I said.

"You know I can't," she said.

"I don't really understand why not."

"That's okay," she said.

We walked to the bus stop and when she saw the bus coming she hugged me.

"Bye baby," she said.

"Bye Mama," I said.

"Maybe I'll come to the States."

"Okay." I hugged her again. "I love you," I said.

"I love you too," she said and kissed me.

I took the bus to the bus terminal and then waited for the bus to Mexico City. I was really tired. When the bus came I sat in my seat and closed my eyes. I imagined my mom on the beach, kneeling on rich people's towels, telling them that the "See you tonight" underwear was her daughter's favorite.

WEEKEND WITH BETH, KELLY, MUSCLE, AND PAMMY

They say men and women can't be friends. Because men will always want to have sex with women, even if we say we don't. We might even think we don't, but if we see the wrong body part in the wrong way, it will be over. Our penises will end us. But I think there's a loophole. If the man in question already had sex with the woman in question and was so drunk that he doesn't remember it. Or he only remembers it enough to know that it was not good. And then the man becomes friends with the woman, and because he has no memory of her vagina, he doesn't think of her as having one. That's what's up with me and my friend Beth. I don't want to sleep with her even though everyone, meaning my sister, Kelly, thinks I do.

I'm also not gay. Which everyone, still meaning my sister, also thinks. That's not why I don't want to sleep with Beth. I'm attracted to women. I'm not attracted to men. But for a straight guy in New York City, I'm not doing such a good job. For a tall guy with almost all of my hair, I am not doing such a good job. I did great in high school. I did fine in the beginning of college. I did horrible later in college and after that I took a break. I've been trying to make a comeback since I got to New York. But New York is weird. And I live with my sister. And back to my sister, the point is she says I have issues. I'm sure I do, just not the lying to myself kind, or the gay kind.

I met Beth the first night of college. We got wasted and had sex. I did two things wrong. Apparently I laughed when she told me to lick her pussy. In my defense, I probably just laughed because I had never heard something like that come out of a girl's mouth. And I had never done that before. I don't know why, but I hadn't. It's probably better that I didn't take my maiden voyage into that salty sea when I was blackout drunk. It turns out that I like it very much, but I found that out too late for Beth. I found that out with Tiffany, which was the other thing I did wrong. When we woke up in the morning, I saw Beth's roommate sleeping in her bed, looking like half Playboy Bunny, half cross-country runner. Which is exactly my type. So I said, "Who's that?" And that was Tiffany.

Beth, on the other hand, wasn't my type. I could see that she was attractive. But I was not attracted to her. At least not when I was sober and had a better sense of how tall she was. I'm six one in shoes but Beth is six two, barefoot. And that morning when I stood up and asked who the blond angel in the other bed was, Beth stood up and told me to get the fuck out. I looked up at her and tried to rearrange my brain. Then I followed her instructions and got the fuck out.

You know the rest of that story. I dated Tiffany. The ratio of times I went down on her to times she went down on me was ten to one. Beth forgave me. We got to be friends. We thought it was funny that we fucked. I was glad I didn't remember it. Tiffany cheated on me with four different guys. A new guy each semester, sophomore and junior years. I never would have found out except I met the guy from spring semester junior year. It was an Italian guy she was fucking in study abroad. I visited her there, in Florence, and we ran into him. Something was lost in translation and he thought I was her brother. He asked if I was as flexible as she was and he laughed. At first I thought it was some kind of compliment. Then I realized something was wrong. When it dawned on me what it was, I punched him in the face and broke his jaw and I told Tiffany I hoped she choked on his dick and died. Either that, or I cried in front of Tiffany and Luca the Italian stallion, and Tiffany broke up with me and put me in a cab to the airport with some napkins. I forget exactly what happened. I honestly thought we were going to get married. That's how fucking stupid I was.

By that time Tiffany and Beth weren't friends anymore. According to Beth, Tiffany was a motherfucking cunt. According to Tiffany, Beth was volatile and had no filter. Tiffany may have been a cheating whore but she was very polite. It drove her nuts that Beth said "pussy" and "retard" and told the chair of the biology department that her biology professor was the worst teacher she had ever had and demanded to know if he even had a PhD. I liked that Beth was rude. It was funny. And her referring to her own vagina as her pussy was disgusting and part of what made our friendship possible.

When we graduated Beth and I got an apartment together in town. I had been offered a job at the college's development office. None of my other friends were staying around. My two best friends fled the country, one to China to teach English and the other to Haiti to be some kind of hero. Beth wanted to stay in town to keep her suspiciously lucrative job at a pizza place. She worked three days a week and she was rich. I asked her more than once if she was sure they were only selling pizza. She said of course they were only selling pizza, expensive pizza. She took home two to three hundred dollars on a regular night, and she always wanted more shifts. One of the girls who worked six days a week drove a brand-new Mercedes and apparently slept with a Yankees player.

Beth got fat that year. She stopped exercising and she didn't know how to cook. Whenever I cooked, she had already called for takeout. She didn't eat at her restaurant because pizza was fattening, so she ordered from the Chinese food place, the Indian place, the Thai place, and the Korean deli down the street from our apartment where everything tasted like Korean food, including the buttered rolls and the brownies.

Beth and I got very comfortable in that apartment. I tried to keep up decorum but she really let it all hang out. By the end of the first week she was walking around in T-shirts and underwear. I had to ask her to put pants on if anyone was stopping by. I still couldn't be sure she was going to. She left clumps of her hair on the walls of the shower. She left tampons bleeding through wads of toilet paper on top of the garbage. She never washed her dishes. We had cockroaches and she didn't care. She talked to them. Like, "You little cocksuckers are getting big. You like that fucking pizza, huh." It was like living with a much grosser but much nicer version of my sister. Or of Tiffany. Or really, a grosser but nicer version of any other girl. Beth gave me a hard time, for sure. But she also wanted to talk to me every day. She brought me pizzas. She watched basketball with me.

So I missed her when I moved to New York. We tried to keep in touch, but she said she was too busy to come to the city. I was too busy to go back down there. We were supposed to celebrate twenty-four together in August. We have the exact same birthday. But when she got to my apartment and I wasn't home, she had a panic attack and drove back to Pennsylvania. My sister was the one who invited her because she said I was lonely. They wanted it to be a surprise. It wasn't, because they kept asking me for each other's phone numbers. Then the real surprise was that Beth didn't show up.

Several weeks later Beth said she was coming to the city to see me. Then she said if I wanted to see her I could meet her and her friend Marnie to go salsa dancing. I did want to see her but not for the price of going salsa dancing. She said she was going to go anyway. I asked her why she told me she was coming to see me if she was really coming to see Marnie. She said I was being a little bitch. She said she knew it wasn't my fault that I was so sensitive but it pissed her off.

I wanted Beth to come see me because I didn't know anyone else. A couple of guys from college worked downtown. I had drinks with them when I first got here. But they weren't close friends and they were hard to track down. Kelly wouldn't let me hang out with her friends.

She was still mad that I slept with her best friend in high school. This girl was unbelievably hot. I never would have gotten to sleep with her if she hadn't been at my house every day of her life, and then decided to let me take care of her when she was drunk and on a shit-ton of mushrooms at a graduation party. The next night she came over to say thank you and that I was the nicest guy ever. And by thank you I mean she let me have sex with her then and several other times that summer. And that is called karma.

So Kelly made it clear that her friends were not my friends. Also because of Kelly, the women in my office thought I was gay, but apparently not the fun kind of gay. Kelly got me a purple shirt to wear on the first day. She knew I would think it was blue because I can't see reds. It never occurred to me that she would do that again. The last time was in high school. She knit me a yellow hat that turned out to be pink. When I got mad at her about the purple shirt she said it didn't matter what color shirt I wore. Everyone knew that all men in development were gay and all women in development were straight. Except for on the finance side, and then the women were also gay. In any case, my coworkers kept to themselves. I spent most of my free time with my sister's dog, Muscle. Other than that I was all alone in the big city. Each night, as I lay under the Brooklyn-Queens Expressway, under the polluted moon, I wept out of loneliness. Ha. Just kidding. But I was really fucking bored.

A month after Beth said she was coming to see me and then didn't, she called. She said she felt bad about the birthday not-surprise and about the salsa dancing, and she was going to visit me for real. I told her I wasn't going to hold my breath in case she couldn't find a parking spot on my street and just kept driving until she got to Canada. She said very funny. She was coming Saturday.

On Saturday morning I made omelets for me and Kelly. Kelly fed half of hers to Muscle. Muscle was a Pomeranian. Kelly shaved him in the summer and it actually did look like he had muscles. But now he had long hair and Kelly called him Pammy because she said he didn't have a penis in the winter. I preferred to call him Pammy year-round because Muscle was a stupid name for a dog. He was very cute and I loved him. He wasn't mean like small dogs are mean. He would just sit and keep you company while you were watching TV or eating dinner or taking a crap or whatever. At night he liked to sleep between Kelly's side and her arm, with his head on her shoulder. When Kelly was out he slept between my side and my arm. He loved to be under the covers except for his head. A tiny, very hairy, yellow person.

Beth called to say that she would be there at one. She got there at twelve forty. Beth had a lead foot. She drove sixty miles an hour in towns, and ninety on the highways.

She drove with her left leg up on the dashboard, her left hand holding a cigarette and resting on the steering wheel. It always seemed likely that I was going to die when I drove with her. One time in particular she was driving seventy through town, on a road full of potholes, and the car sounded like it was losing big pieces. I was absolutely certain I was going to die. She called me a pussy for holding on to the door.

I let Beth in and she gave me a big hug and said, "I love those slippers more and more every day." My mom gave me these shearling slippers when Tiffany broke up with me and I was spending a lot of time in my dorm room. Now they were full of holes. It felt good to see Beth.

Since I hadn't known if she was going to show up, I hadn't made any plans. Now I was thinking we could take a long walk with Pammy. Talk about life and internet dating. Get sandwiches and eat in the park. Watch a game and cook something healthy, something that Beth could learn from without me explicitly teaching her. I tried to do that when we lived together, to indeterminate effect. When I moved out I thought I'd be glad not to have to take care of her. Now I kind of missed it. At least she showed some appreciation. My sister showed none.

"What should we do?" I asked Beth, thinking she would say, "Whatever you want."

"Shopping!" she said. I had never known Beth to want to go shopping before. Fine, I could do shopping. Beth said she wanted jeans and stuff for yoga and a perfume sample for a girl she worked with. Kelly said she couldn't come because she had work to do, but she made a list of stores for us to go to in SoHo. When we left she was taking turns putting coats of paint on her nails and her dog's nails.

"I think nail polish is toxic for dogs," said Beth.

"This is dog nail polish," said Kelly. It was yellow and Pammy was licking it.

"What do you two want to do for dinner?" I said.

"Something free," said Kelly.

"What, I buy you dinner?" I said.

"Oh would you?" She smiled.

"Let's cook here," I said.

"Sure," said Beth.

"You know what I feel like? Diner-style grilled cheese and french fries and root beer," said Kelly. So much for teaching Beth how to make something healthy.

"Fine with me," I said. "Beth?"

"Sure."

On the way to the subway Beth and I went into a store with crafts and stuff. I tried to wait outside but Beth wanted to try on all the jewelry and have me tell her how it looked. I thought all the jewelry looked the same. The crafts looked like stuff that Kelly's friends made, maybe worse.

Beth bought a ring. We looked in a junk shop next to the subway station and then got on the train. We sat down next to a deaf couple who were signing to each other and laughing hysterically.

"What's been going on?" said Beth.

"Not much," I said. "Work, bad dates, work."

"Bad dates," she said. "There's no way your dates are as bad as my dates." She told me about this guy who was a regular at the restaurant. He turned out to be married with kids but took his wedding ring off when he went there to eat lunch. She said she didn't like being the other woman but she couldn't stop. Before that there was another guy. Her age, but a socially conservative Republican. They couldn't talk to each other about anything but they also didn't need to. They were always having sex. Then it turned out that he was not actually her age. He was still in college. He was the head of the campus conservatives, a group that we had not taken seriously when we went there.

Back when we lived together I would have given her a lecture about both of these guys. Now I didn't know what to say. It wasn't like the lectures had worked. All of Beth's lovers were basically the same. Good in bed but deeply morally flawed. In college she had been less discriminating, but she had developed this particular taste in the last four years. It seemed like she thought good men and good sex were mutually exclusive. They probably had been back in college. Good guys didn't know what they were doing, and bad guys did. I didn't do an anthropological study on this or anything. But I know that I thought I knew what I was doing and I definitely didn't. The one nice thing that Tiffany did for me was to tell me that I didn't know what I was doing, although I have never been more ashamed in my life. And obviously I didn't improve quickly enough to not get cheated on. But Tiffany taught me that you have to assume you know nothing. I do think that makes me better in bed. At least less arrogant. Basically this is the most embarrassing thing I've ever thought about.

I didn't want to talk to Beth about sex, but I did want to tell her about the girls I had been meeting on the internet. I wanted to ask her if she thought I had tried hard enough and could give up. I had been on eleven first dates and two second dates. I had sex with two of the first-date girls. The first girl I wouldn't have slept with, except her grandma died between when we were e-mailing and when we got together. When she halfheartedly suggested we go back to her place, I felt like I should take her up on it. I pretended I was really into it. There wasn't anything wrong with her. But nothing made me feel drawn to her, other than how cheerful she was trying to be despite obviously being so sad. It ended up being very high energy, very good sex. But we both understood that that was that. The second girl I had higher hopes for. The sex was good in a more routine way, but I think she dated a lot. My friends might have called her a slut, but I didn't have any friends. And when I was in high school my mom sat me down to talk about the word "slut" and to give me a general lecture about how to make her proud despite my being a man.

That girl never called me back. But before I could talk to Beth about any of this, we got to SoHo.

Beth wanted to go to the jeans store first. She tried on about a hundred pairs. She didn't like the way any of them looked because she was still a little bit fat.

"This brand does not fit well at all," she said. "Maybe they fit Kelly but she's a lot shorter than me."

Because Beth was thin and then fat and now almost thin again, it was like she didn't remember being fat. She didn't even act fat when she was fat. When we were living together she found out she had high cholesterol and said, "But I thought that was for fat people."

We left the store and walked down Greene Street. Beth grabbed my arm and took a couple of bouncy steps.

"If I lived in New York, I would live in SoHo," she said.

"Oh really," I said. "Do you even know how much apartments here are?"

"They're expensive, huh?"

"They're like four grand for a hundred square feet." Sometimes Beth seemed to know nothing about how the world worked.

"Well I like it here, it's my favorite neighborhood."

"What other neighborhoods have you been to?"

"I don't know."

"You can't even walk down the sidewalk, there are so many people. I like my neighborhood."

"I like your neighborhood too. Calm down. I don't not like your neighborhood. I just like this neighborhood too."

"Fine," I said. "Live here when you move to the city."

"Maybe I will," she said.

The sporting goods store didn't really have any sporting goods. Unless you think stretchy clothes that cost more than a nice steak and a bottle of wine are sporting goods.

I looked at the men's clothes. When I got to the back of the store Beth was freaking out about some underwear. The girl who was helping her was looking through a rack of bras and Beth was jumping up and down.

"These bras and shorts are special for hot yoga," she said.

"Those are shorts?"

"Oh my god, I'm so excited." She took a bunch of things back to the dressing room.

I sat in the most comfortable chair ever.

"What kind of chair is this?" I asked a different girl, who was putting hangers on clothes at a table.

"What?" When she turned around I realized she was gorgeous. She had huge blue eyes and she was tiny. She looked like a little elf but without pointy ears and with a really nice body. The stretchy clothes fit her like a dream.

"Never mind," I said. "It doesn't matter."

"What kind of chair is it? Do you want me to find out?" She had a killer smile, her teeth were perfect.

"No, that's okay," I said. "I don't know why I said that. I don't need a chair." I smiled at her.

"Jason?" said Beth. "Do you want to see this stuff or not?"

"Uh," I said.

"I love love love this stuff." She opened the dressing room door and came out wearing a bra and the so-called shorts.

"Please tell me you don't go to yoga like that," I said.

Beth's hair was coming out of the sides of the underwear. There was a lot of it. Once we reached the point where no amount of information was too much information, except any information about me having sex with Tiffany, Beth told me that the place she went to get waxed charged her extra. I mean I used to see her in underwear all the time. But now it was at eye level. It was not a good surprise. And it caused some involuntary stirring, which made everything worse.

"Of course I do." She stuck her tongue out and let it hang there. She turned around and went back into the room.

"Tell your girlfriend I'll be right back if she needs another size," said the beautiful elf.

I started to say, "She's not my girlfriend," but only got as far as "Sh—"

"Thanks!" Beth said through the door.

Beth came out. Another girl came over to take the things she didn't want. Beth handed her everything.

"What are you getting?" I said.

"I don't think anything," said Beth.

"What? Why not?"

She shrugged. "I don't know, I just don't want to get anything."

"Okay," I said. On the way out I smiled at the elf. Beth rolled her eyes and said it was lame how I hit on her by asking about the chair.

"I wasn't hitting on her," I said.

"Oh please, Jason. I would recognize your lame moves through a brick wall."

"I swear. I didn't even see that she was hot until after I said the thing about the chair."

"Whatever," said Beth.

"Where do you want to go next?" I said.

"I think I'm fucking getting my period," she said. "I need a cupcake or something."

We went to a gourmet store where I once accidentally got a cup of yogurt and granola for eleven dollars before an interview.

"I think I want a cookie," I said.

"Me too," she said.

We decided to split one peanut butter and one ginger.

After we paid we stood at the counter eating them. The peanut butter cookie was crunchy.

"Damn," I said. "It looked like it was going to be soft."

Beth took a bite of hers and chewed carefully. "It's probably old."

"What? Why would it be old?"

"Because it's crunchy."

"Crunchy cookies can be not old," I said.

"I don't think so," said Beth. "No."

Next we went to some special store that only had one kind of perfume. Beth's friend ordered a sample and it never came, so Beth wanted to get it for her.

The girl handed Beth a tiny vial, and Beth said, "It's fifteen dollars, right?"

"Wait, what?" I said.

"It's complimentary," said the girl.

"Oh my god, really?" said Beth. "Thank you so much."

"Sure," said the girl. "Have a good day."

We left and Beth put the sample in her bag.

"Tell me you weren't just going to pay fifteen dollars for that," I said.

"Yeah I was," said Beth.

"Beth, come on. They give those out at every store. Kelly has like a hundred in the bathroom."

"I know, but this one was supposed to be fifteen dollars, Camille said so."

"There's no way," I said. "Come on, please be smart about this stuff."

"Well Camille really wanted it," said Beth. "She waited for it to come in the mail for a month."

Beth was really killing me. I couldn't even look at her on the way to the grocery store. She didn't notice. We had had moments like this before. But today I felt really out of patience and I didn't know why. I was supposed to be Mr. Patient. I would wait for you to stop cheating on me for years and years if you needed me to. That's how fucking patient I am. When we got to the grocery store Beth said she wasn't that hungry, and I wasn't really either.

We had a fight about whether to get rustic bread and cheddar cheese or white bread and American cheese, and finally Beth decided she wasn't going to eat grilled cheese anyway. She only wanted to eat fruit for dinner. So I bought the white and American, frozen french fries, and a six-pack of sugar-free root beer for Kelly. Beth bought a fruit salad and at the last minute, some dumplings.

The subway didn't come for a long time. Neither of us was over our fight about the grilled cheese yet. Beth pointed out the rats running around the tracks like she was glad to see them. I missed that about her. Right before Tiffany's semester in Italy, Tiffany and I stayed on a houseboat in Berlin. It was full of spiders. There were ten or twenty spiders on every surface. The bunk beds. The table. The chairs. Our suitcases. Our shoes. At least two or three hundred total. I counted more than eighty as I threw them out the window. I was sliding them onto pieces of paper and brushing them off into the water. It seemed like as many as I was throwing out were coming back in through the open window and under the door. Tiffany sat on the top bunk, whimpering and flicking any she could see with her long nails. Until she saw the webs on the ceiling, only a foot or two from her head. Her scream shook the boat. If I had been a spider I would have jumped out the window voluntarily. Instead I caught her arm as she threw herself off the bed. I hugged her and kissed her. That night was the last time we had sex. Tiff gave me an amazing blow job. She said it was because I saved her from the spiders, but I think it was because she knew it was the last time.

Beth and I watched the rats in silence until the subway came. On the subway Beth said, "So, what about your bad dates?"

"Oh," I said. "You know. New York is weird."

"You should go back and ask that girl out."

"What girl?" I said.

In a deep voice Beth said, "What kind of chair is this? It's really comfortable but I bet it's not as comfortable as your vagina."

The old man across the aisle looked up at us.

I started to laugh. Beth started too. We cracked up for

a minute. Then we stopped. We didn't really have anything else to say.

When we got home, Kelly was making lanterns out of jam jars and wire and hanging them on the fire escape with candles in them.

"That's so beautiful," said Beth.

"Thanks," said Kelly. "I hope they're sturdy."

"How do you know if they're sturdy or not?" said Beth.

"I don't," said Kelly.

"Well they're beautiful," said Beth. "I'm very impressed."

"Thanks." Kelly smiled.

I let Beth ask Kelly a million questions about lanterns and beaded chandeliers and stripping furniture. Since Kelly was Kelly, it was a win-win situation. I put the french fries in and constructed the grilled cheese. I wondered what to do about Beth's dumplings.

"Do you want me to warm up your dumplings?"

"Yeah baby, warm up my dumplings," she said. "No, I like to eat them cold."

When everything was ready she got them out of the fridge and started eating them out of the package. Then she went to the cabinet and took a glass down and held it up to the light and put it in the sink. She took another and did the same thing.

"Beth," I said.

"What?"

"Are you putting our glasses in the sink because they're not clean enough?"

"Yeah, should I not?"

"No, you should not. It's rude."

"Oh, is it?" said Beth, not sarcastically. "My mom does it to me."

"That's different. That's your mom."

"Okay. What should I do?"

"If you don't see one that looks good then wash one."

"Okay," she said and washed a glass.

Kelly came in and we sat down to eat. Beth asked where the forks were and I got up to get her one.

"Is this clean enough for you?" I said.

Beth inspected it. "Yes."

"Jason is mad at me because I put some dirty glasses in the sink," she said to Kelly.

"Why is that bad?" said Kelly.

"Not from the counter," I said, "from the cabinet."

"Oh," said Kelly. "Well that's probably my fault. I think I did dishes last."

It was definitely Kelly's fault. She did dishes like she was blind and also had no fingers. There was always dried orange juice pulp on the glasses.

After dinner Kelly got dressed and went out. Beth and I watched a basketball game. I worked on a proposal letter. When the game ended I opened the futon for Beth and gave her a pillow and a blanket. I brought Pammy into my room, closed the door, got into bed, and jerked off.

The next morning I woke up early by accident. I took Pammy out for a run. On our way out he licked Beth's feet, which were hanging off the futon. Beth's feet were like everything else about her. Oversized but fine. She didn't have anything gross like bunions and her toes were the right length and right width. I started to pay attention to this in high school because the only thing I could say to Kelly that really upset her was that her feet were ugly. They were and she knew it. And then in college I turned into kind of a foot guy. Tiffany's feet were sexy. They were tiny and she had perfectly shaped toenails, like little shells. She had them done all the time and sometimes I did them for her. She told somebody about that, probably one of the guys she was fucking. My friends asked me if I wiped her ass for her, too.

I have all my epiphanies when I'm running. I had three contradictory epiphanies on the run with Pammy. I needed one more epiphany to tell me what the real epiphany was. The three options were: 1. The reason I didn't want to sleep with Beth wasn't because she kind of grossed me out, or because I didn't really want to sleep with anyone after Tiffany the life-wrecking whore, but because she was like a sister to me, which explained all the fighting. 2. I actually did want to sleep with her, which also explained all the fighting. Or 3. We didn't actually have anything in common, and I neither wanted to sleep with nor be friends with her.

I wanted it to be number 1 so that we could still be friends, and I didn't want it to be number 3. As for number 2, I really didn't think I wanted to sleep with her. Although I would have liked for her to know that I was better in bed now. And it would have made sense if the inverse of us hating each other all day was fucking each other all night. And I really did want to have sex. But I just didn't want to do it with Beth.

I gave up trying to figure it out. Instead I thought about how I had too many women in my life. Too many women and all the wrong kind.

On the way back from the run, Pammy and I went to the bodega to get buttermilk and eggs to make pancakes. Beth was still asleep on the couch. I let Pammy into Kelly's room and I measured ingredients in the kitchen. When the girls still weren't up I opened my proposal letter but then played Minesweeper instead.

I heard Beth get up and go into the bathroom. Then she came into my room and said, "What's cooking, good-looking?"

"I was going to make pancakes," I said. "Are you hungry?"

"Sure," she said. "Is Kelly up?"

"No, but she sleeps forever," I said.

We went into the kitchen. I mixed everything up and heated the griddle.

Beth washed berries. We put them in the pancakes. When Beth was looking through a drawer for a spatula she found a bone-shaped cookie cutter. She put it on the griddle and made a pancake for Pammy.

Kelly got up when the pancakes were ready. She is psychic about food. "Aw," she said when she saw the bone pancake. "That is so cute. I love that you love my little Muscle-wuscle."

"I don't know if I love him," said Beth. "I just thought it would be funny."

Kelly looked hurt. I laughed.

They sat down to eat. I made more pancakes. After breakfast Kelly left and Beth helped me do the dishes.

"I'm sorry about yesterday," she said.

"Me too," I said.

"Are you still mad about the glasses?"

"No. It was just a weird day."

"I know," she said.

"It's not my fault the glasses were dirty. Kelly can't do dishes to save her life."

I hadn't planned on throwing my sister under the bus. I wanted to take it back.

"Okay," said Beth.

I was ready for the weekend to be over. But I had

already asked Beth to take me to the store to get paper towels and toilet paper, so she did. When we got back she parked four feet from the curb. She got out to open her trunk for me.

"Thanks for taking me to get these things," I said.

"Of course."

"Have a safe trip home."

"I will. Let's do this again soon?" She gave me a hug.

"Sure," I said. I didn't think it would be soon.

"All right," she said. "Back to my crappy fucking life."

She got into her car and lit a cigarette and peeled into the street. The car turned out of sight at the end of the block.

I went inside. I tried to work on my computer in bed. But it was hard to keep my eyes open. Pammy came in and got under the covers. We slept for a long time.

MIKE ANONYMOUS

When Mike Anonymous first called the clinic they made me pick up the phone. I didn't know what the hell he was saying so I put him on hold. They always made me pick up when someone with an Asian accent called, like I could speak a word of any Asian language, which I couldn't. This guy was actually Japanese, I could tell that much. I was a quarter Japanese, but my Japanese grandma died when I was five, and I had never been able to understand her either.

Mike Anonymous was the fourth caller on hold, which was the maximum, so at least all the lines were busy and the phones were going to stop ringing. It was my lunch break but I was sitting at the security window, and people kept calling and coming in and needing things. I was looking out the front door straight into the sun. I wished I had sunglasses or ski goggles or something. Every time someone opened the door, cold air rushed through and made me shudder.

Louisa was wearing her coat at the check-in desk, but she kept asking me what was wrong with me, like I shouldn't be freezing my ass off. Finally I was like, "Fat people get cold too," and she cracked up.

I picked up line one but the caller was gone, and the phone started ringing again.

"Hello, thank you for calling Gonorrheaville, would you mind holding just a minute?" Louisa pressed the hold button.

"Oh my god," I laughed. "What if someone from administration calls and you say that?"

"They'd call the private line."

"What if they didn't?" I said.

"They definitely wouldn't call the patient line. They know we don't pick it up."

"We try to pick it up."

I picked up line four and it was still the guy I couldn't understand.

Something something HIV, he said.

"Do you want to make an appointment?"

Something something HIV, he said again.

"Do you want to be tested for STDs?"

Something something, he said in a high voice.

"Sex-u-ally trans-mit-ted dis-ea-ses?" I said.

"Yes!"

The private line started ringing.

"Okay, hold on," I said, and picked up the private line.

"Viv?" It was my stupid boyfriend Davey. "What time are you coming home?"

I hung up the phone and wondered if Davey definitely knew it was me who picked up.

I picked up line four. "Okay, what's your name?"

Something something anonymous, he said.

"You want to be anonymous?" I said. "Fine, but you have to have a first name. What's your first name?"

"Ano . . . Mike-des," he said.

"Mike Dess?"

"Mike!"

"Okay, Mike. Do you have any symptoms?"

It sounded like Mike Anonymous didn't have any symptoms, so I made an appointment for an STD testing with no symptoms at seven the next night. I ate the last bite of my eighth brown rice cake with peanut butter and went back to work.

The next day Louisa had to work the front desk with Boss Donna, so she answered the phones, "Thank you for calling the clinic, this is Louisa, how can I help you?" instead of "Gonorrheaville, please hold," or her other favorite, "Chlamydialand."

I was in the dirty lab getting instruments out of the autoclave when Donna paged me. "Vivian to the front, please. Vivian to the front." Boss Donna loved the intercom.

I walked to the front, stepping on only the pink tiles.

"Your patient is here," Donna said when I got there. "The one that called yesterday."

"What?" I said. The waiting room was empty except for a man filling out paperwork in the closest seat to the check-in window. He was sweating and his face was flushed. He looked like he was in his thirties or forties. He wasn't fat-fat but he had a round face and he filled out his suit.

"That guy?" I said.

"No, one of the other guys," said Donna. "Yes, that guy."

I shut the window between the check-in desk and the waiting room.

"He speaks no English," said Louisa, "not one word."

"That's Mike Anonymous?" I said. "He's not supposed to be here until seven. How come he's my patient?"

"Because we can't understand him at all," said Louisa.

"Neither can I!" I said.

"We'll let you know when his chart is ready," said Donna.

His chart was ready quickly because he didn't answer

any of the questions on the questionnaire. I brought him back to the bathroom to pee in a cup and told him to leave the cup in the window and meet me in the lab. But when he came into the lab he was holding his urine cup. He was still sweating. I smiled at him but he didn't smile back.

He sat in the blood-drawing chair and I asked him all of the questions he hadn't answered. I rephrased them so that he could answer yes or no. His breathing got heavier and he answered the questions in gasps. When I got to the questions about who he had sex with and how, he said yes to being married. He didn't answer how he had sex, and I wasn't about to ask yes-or-no questions about whether he had oral, vaginal, or anal, so I skipped that part. He shook his head like he didn't understand again when I asked him whether he had had more than one sex partner in the last six months. Two drops of sweat fell onto his shirt. I wondered if it was possible that he understood me perfectly.

"We'll test your urine for gonorrhea and chlamydia and your blood for HIV," I said.

He took some gauze from the supply table and dabbed his chin and then his forehead. Now I was pretty sure he actually had no idea what I was saying. I pricked his finger for the rapid HIV test, set the timer, and sent him back out to the waiting room.

. . .

I started working at the clinic after I graduated from college. I was supposed to do some other stuff, like med school, but I kind of crashed and burned in the fall semester of my senior year, and now I was trying to figure out what to do about my life.

My childhood dream was to be a girl-scientist. I started conducting chemistry experiments in the kitchen before I could read. My parents gave me a drawer to keep my potions in, and the only rules were that I couldn't use anything with a green Mr. Yuk sticker on it, and I couldn't use anything from the garage. In first grade, my half brother Charlie got sick, and I imagined that if one of my potions cured him, I would be such a famous girl-scientist that I would have to wear disguises when I went outside. I made more and more potions, and when Charlie came to visit he tried the ones I picked out for him. He took a tiny sip from each, and once he threw up from smelling one.

Charlie was eighteen years older than I was, and he lived in New York City. I remember thinking that he was the person who knew me best in the world, because he sent me fancy dresses for every holiday except Halloween, when he sent me costumes. Later my mom told me that he bought them at a special store and cut out the tags, but at the time I thought he made them for me. My mom said she told him to stop sending them because she knew he couldn't afford them, but he didn't care what he could afford. When my dad sent him money for food and bills, he used it to buy dresses, records, and pieces of china for his Royal Copenhagen collection, which he left to me.

After that, I started thinking I might become a girl-doctor instead of a girl-scientist. I thought that through high school and most of college. And now I was supposed to be applying for something for next year, but I didn't know what. I didn't know if I still had it in me to study medicine, or even chemistry. I was thinking I might want to study public health, but I was also thinking I might want to move to the forest and eat berries and mushrooms and hibernate with the bears in the winter.

Mike Anonymous's test was negative. I called him back in. His shirt around his neck and under his armpits was see-through with sweat. I showed him to the closest counseling room. I could hear him breathing as he went into the room in front of me and sat down, and I told him it was negative before the door even closed, because I thought he was going to pass out if I didn't. But instead of being glad, Mike Anonymous stood up and slammed his hand on the table and said, "No!" I jumped. Then I think he said the test was wrong, or I did the test wrong. He wanted the traditional test, and he wanted to see a doctor. I was starting to understand him better but I was also starting to get scared of him. I told him he couldn't see a doctor unless he had symptoms, and he said he did have symptoms.

"You told me on the phone you didn't have symptoms," I said.

"No," he said.

"Okay fine," I said, "what are your symptoms?"

He showed me a dot on his hand that looked like a freckle but was black.

"Are you sure that's not ink?" I said.

"What?" he said.

"Ink," I said, "like pen?"

Mike Anonymous shook his head and waved his hand in my face so that I could get a better look at the symptom.

"Okay," I said. "Anything else?"

Something something penis, he said.

"Something is wrong with your penis?" I said.

Something something penis, he said again, louder. I told him to hold on and went out to the hall. A med student had arrived with Dr. Wagner, and they were talking to the clinicians about what patient to take.

"I have a really good patient for you," I said.

The med student looked excited, like he thought it was going to be a woman with a double vagina or something. He was new to the clinic and he was technically a resident, which allowed him to see patients under Dr. Wagner's guidance. He was too tall and he walked like it was hard for him to balance on such long legs. I wondered if that was why Dr. Wagner didn't seem to take him seriously.

"This guy is sure he's HIV positive but he had a negative rapid test, and when I told him it was negative, he decided that something was wrong with his penis," I told them.

The med student still looked excited but Dr. Wagner rolled her eyes.

"Why does he think he's HIV positive?" she said.

"I don't know," I said.

"Don't you think you should find out?" she said.

"Um," I said.

I went back to the counseling room and told Mike that a doctor would see him, but first I needed to know why he thought he was HIV positive. He just looked at me, rasping now, and I made a mental note to offer him some water later. I sat down and wondered what to ask him and why I hadn't been trained to do this.

"Have you ever used needles to take drugs?" I said.

"No."

"Have you ever had sex with another man?"

"No!"

I tried to think of the other HIV risk factors.

"Have you ever exchanged sex for money?"

Mike Anonymous started to shake. He shook harder and harder and then he started to sob and talk. I had no idea what words he was saying, but at the end I made out the words "my kids." I didn't know what to do. I took a box of tissues from the file cabinet and put it on the table.

"I'm sorry," I said.

He looked at me and hiccupped.

"Did you have sex with a prostitute?"

"Yes," he said.

"Did you use protection? A condom?"

"It has broken."

He suddenly seemed very calm and I wondered if this was when he was going to pass out. I watched him for a minute. I wondered if he was a researcher at the university or something. I couldn't think of another explanation for a man with nice shoes and a nice bag and a wife and kids, who could barely speak English, and who either could or could not understand it.

"Okay," I said. "I'm going to go get the doctor."

He nodded.

"Will you be okay here if I leave for a second?"

He nodded again.

I still didn't want to leave him so I stuck my foot in the door and called down the hall, hoping that Dr. Wagner was down there.

"What?" she called back.

"Can you come up here?" I said.

"What?" she said.

"Can you please come to counseling room one?"

When she and the resident got there I looked at Mike

and he seemed okay, so I closed the door and told Dr. Wagner about the hooker. She asked what exam room they could use and I told her room two. I gave her his chart.

"He can't be anonymous if we're going to examine him," she said.

"You're going to have to find out his name," said the resident. I decided he wasn't speaking to me since he was so tall. I opened the door to the counseling room and Mike Anonymous looked at us.

"Mike, this is Dr. Wagner," I said. "She's going to take care of you."

Mike nodded.

"Hi, I'm Dr. Phillips." The resident smiled and I wanted to kick his spider legs out from under him.

I brought Mike a cup of water and moved him to the exam room. They were in there for forty minutes, or the amount of time that it took Judy and Eunice, the other clinicians, to see six patients. When Dr. Wagner came out she ordered a herpes 2 test and a hepatitis C test.

"What was wrong with his penis?" I said.

"Nothing," said Dr. Wagner. "He doesn't have a single symptom."

The resident handed me Mike's chart and a requisition form for the tests, and then he repeated the names of the tests, like he thought of them himself. He had filled out the requisition form wrong and ordered a herpes culture instead of a herpes blood test, so I pointed that out to him.

I brought Mike Anonymous back into the lab and drew blood to send out. He wanted me to order a second HIV test from the lab, so I asked Dr. Wagner if I could. She said yes because it was the only way to get him to shut up about how he was HIV positive and the first test couldn't tell because it couldn't pick up the antibodies in Asian blood.

"What?" I said. "That's crazy."

"Is it?" said Dr. Wagner to the resident. "What do you know about that?"

"I can find out more," said the resident. "I'll make a call."

"Are you retarded?" said Dr. Wagner. "Did you even go to med school?"

"I know," said the resident. "I was just joking."

Davey called at three to make sure I was getting off of work at four and could help him cut the dog's nails. He said they were clicking on the floor and if we didn't cut them at four he wouldn't be able to get any work done for the whole rest of the day. I swore on the book of skin diseases that if he called me on the private line one more time I was going to break up with him. When I hung up, my coworker Pregnant Patricia asked me if I could stay late for her, because she had to go to an emergency doctor's appointment that she had been waiting a month to get. I told her I could. I called Davey back and left a message so that he wouldn't come to the clinic right at four with the dog and the nail clippers. I said the baby inside of Patricia had a life-or-death situation and I had no choice but to stay until eight.

After Patricia, Boss Donna, and Louisa left at four, Louisa called to tell me that Patricia had lied and was really going to a job interview. Before Pregnant Patricia was Pregnant Patricia she was Fat Patricia, because she was fatter than anyone else, even me. Fat Patricia and the women who had been working at the clinic for four years or six years or eleven years sent out their resumes from the fax machine whenever Boss Donna was out of the office, but no one had gotten a new job in the ten months I had worked there. Even though I was going to leave the job and hopefully the city and the state when my lease was up in two months, I imagined myself doing STD screenings when I was seventy. If I gained five pounds a year eating the donuts that the drug reps brought, I would be enormous by then.

A little before seven, Mike Anonymous came back with a woman. She was tall and black and didn't look like I would have expected her to look, if I had expected to see her. She had perfect teeth and perfect skin, and she had purplish-blue contacts.

Mike said he had an appointment. I was starting to understand his accent well enough. I looked at Melissa, who was working the front desk with me.

"You were already here," I said to Mike.

Mike said he wanted to give the woman his appointment, and when I said we canceled it, he said she would wait for a same-day appointment.

"I ain't waiting," the woman said.

"Hang on," I said.

I went to the back and asked Eunice what to do. She looked at the clock. We had to take walk-ins until seven and it was six fifty-four.

"Fuck," she said.

Back at the front, I gave the woman an intake form and an STD questionnaire, and she filled them out with her back to Mike. Melissa entered her into the computer and I put her chart together and brought her in.

Her name was Marla Jones. Marla Jones looked like she was twenty but the birthday in her chart made her thirty-eight. She wasn't wearing makeup and she wasn't wearing a miniskirt. She was wearing jeans and a puffy coat.

Marla had answered all of the questions in loopy handwriting. I asked her the standard counseling questions, like whether she was ready to get a negative or positive result in fifteen minutes, and what she would do either way. The only question that wasn't standard was whether she felt like she was being forced to get tested, which we asked when patients were with their moms, and which seemed relevant now.

"I ain't being forced," she said, "I'm getting paid."

I started the test and put Marla in a counseling room. I didn't want to send her back out to wait with Mike Anonymous. When I got back to the lab, Eunice and Melissa were standing over the test. They made room for me and we all waited for the lines to come up. It worked like a pregnancy test: one line was good, two lines were bad.

The control line came up and then the positive line came up. Two lines.

I felt like air was rushing through my head. I sat down in the blood-drawing chair.

"Dear God," said Eunice.

"I feel sick," said Melissa. She left the lab.

"I need a minute," said Eunice. She went back out to the clinician's station and put her head in her hands.

Soon I stopped feeling dizzy and felt empty, like this wasn't real life, which was a relief. When Eunice was ready I followed her into the counseling room. Marla didn't look up from her magazine.

"Marla? Hi, I'm Eunice."

"Hi."

"Hi." Eunice sat down. "Are you ready for your results?"

"Yeah," said Marla.

"Your HIV test was positive," said Eunice.

"Yeah," said Marla. She didn't look up.

"Okay," said Eunice. "Did you already know that you might be HIV positive?"

"Yeah," said Marla.

"Are you currently under a physician's care?" said Eunice.

"No," said Marla. She looked up.

I gave Marla a card for the hospital's AIDS care program. Eunice asked her how she was going to deal with her results tonight and tomorrow, and asked her about her support network, but Marla kept saying she was fine. Eunice told her that we were going to report the result under our mandated reporting protocol. She wanted to do a confirmation test before Marla left, but Marla said it was already confirmed.

"Okay," said Eunice. "Will you call the program?"

"Uh-huh," said Marla. "I got to go."

"Okay," said Eunice. "We'll call you tomorrow to see how you're doing."

I walked Marla to the checkout desk. Mike Anonymous was waiting for her on the other side of the door.

"He's paying," she said. She opened the door to the waiting room and told Mike Anonymous that he needed to pay and that he owed her fifty bucks. He said he needed the results first.

"Hell no," she said.

He said he was paying her so she had to give him the results.

"No," said Marla. She walked past him.

He said that was the agreement.

"Okay," said Marla. "Give me the money first."

He handed her some cash and she started walking toward the door.

"Hey!" he said. But instead of following her, Mike Anonymous stormed our window, yelling that he needed the results.

"I think you should shut that," I said to Melissa.

She closed the window, and we watched Mike yelling on the other side. He was yelling that we had to give him the results because he paid for the test and it was his money, so they were his results.

"We can't give you the results," I said through the glass. "It's against the law." I didn't tell him that he hadn't paid yet.

He was sweating again and he was crying. He yelled that he knew it was positive. Then he really started screaming, not words but just screaming. He ran into a row of chairs, knocking them over and falling on top of them.

I picked up the phone and pressed page. "I think we need help up here."

By the time Eunice got to the front, Mike Anonymous had taken a couple of pictures off the wall and pulled down a set of track lights.

"Do you want me to call the police?" I said. We watched him through the window. He looked weaker. He knocked over the pamphlet display in slow motion and then sat down on a chair and put his head between his knees.

"Call them if I wave at you," said Eunice. "I'm going to take him outside."

She went out to the waiting room and took his elbow and helped him stand up. We watched her escort him outside. She looked older, like his red face set off her gray hair.

They left the building and walked across the parking lot. The streetlights lit them up and made shadows under their eyes and noses and chins. We could see Mike Anonymous shaking and shouting and then calming down again. Eunice tightened her grip on him and then loosened it. It made me want to cry that this old lady was showing him what was what.

She led him to a bench and activated the safety light on the side of the building. She had on her calmest face, but she was shivering. I wondered if I should bring her her coat but I didn't want to interrupt. Mike put his head down again and Eunice talked to him, and I could hear her voice in my head. Her voice was very soothing and she had been the only clinician I wasn't afraid of when I started working at the clinic.

Mike didn't get worked up again, so Melissa and I closed the exam rooms and Melissa did the deposit and

I put the pamphlet display back together and left a message for maintenance about the pictures and the track lights. When we were almost ready to go Eunice came back in alone and said that Mike Anonymous would be back in three months for a follow-up test.

When I got home Davey was mad about me working late and he made me help him clip the dog's nails right away, before I had a chance to pee or open a bottle of wine.

"How was work?" he said, but it sounded like he meant, *I hate you for fucking up my day.*

"It was fine," I said, hoping it sounded like, *I hate you for fucking up my life.*

I made cereal for dinner and Davey played Call of Duty. When I told him I was going to bed he waved at me, and then later he tried to wake me up to have sex with him. I was pretty asleep but I figured if we did it then, we wouldn't have to do it while I was awake, and he would leave me alone for at least a week.

When he got on top of me the dog went under the covers. Davey was taking a long time to come and while he was working on it, I decided to tell him.

"I don't want to live here anymore," I said.

"Fuck," he said. "That fucking dog is licking my feet. What did you say?"

"Nothing," I said.

"Vivian, what?" he said.

I pushed him out of me and closed my legs. "We had an HIV positive today."

He tried to separate my legs again. "Don't you have HIV positives all the time?"

"No. We never have HIV positives."

I moved over and put my underwear back on.

I WILL CRAWL TO
RALEIGH IF I HAVE TO

My mom and I were going to stop to break up with my boyfriend on our way to Emerald Isle, but the muffler fell off of my car right before we got to the exit we needed to take to Raleigh, and my mom said we couldn't stop anymore. I was driving, and I had been waiting for this exit for three hours, since we left home. I started crying and for a while I was crying so hard I could barely see. The car was so loud that I could barely hear either, and my mom was trying to talk to me but I didn't care because I was mad at her for not letting us stop. Finally she got in my face and yelled, "PULL! OVER!" so I did and we switched seats. I cried for at least ten more minutes, which was more tears than it sounds like. My mom shouted over the noise that it was okay because we would get the car fixed when we got to Emerald Isle and I could stop in Raleigh to break up with James on the way back. I yelled that my vacation was ruined.

We had no choice but to spend the next three hours in silence, or obviously not in silence but not saying anything. My mom drove in the right lane. She put on her sunglasses and tried to ignore all the cars passing us and staring.

I had insisted on taking my car because I didn't want it to look like my mom drove me to break up with my boyfriend. My plan had been to drop her off near James's house and pick her up when I was done, but now all my plans had gone to shit.

When we finally got to Emerald Isle, my mom's boyfriend, Mak, was unloading beer from his car, and my brother, Noah, was on a walk with the dog, meaning he was smoking weed somewhere and letting Petey chew on rocks. The three of them had left Virginia at the crack of dawn that morning because Mak was in a big hurry to get to North Carolina to play golf. My mom and I had waited to get our hair and nails done, because my mom wanted to look good for her boyfriend's brother's wife, and because I wanted to look good for when I turned single.

We were renting a house with Mak and Mak's brother's family, the Henderchenkos. They were the Henderchenkos because Mak's brother used to be "Boychenko" and his wife used to be "Henderson," and by combining they saved themselves six letters and a hyphen.

The house was smaller and crappier than I had imagined when my mom said we were getting a nice big house for everyone. There were only three bedrooms, and I guessed I was sharing with my brother, which left my mom and Mak in the second bedroom, and the Henderchenkos—Andy, Tina, and their son, Dylan—in the third. Unless Dylan was sharing with me and Noah, but I didn't think my mom and Mak would do that to us.

We had been on Emerald Isle at the same time as the Henderchenkos for the past several years, but we had never shared a house. I liked them fine, but they were very serious people. They were always dressed up, even at the beach. Tina wasn't as pretty as my mom, but she worked much harder at being pretty, and that somehow made my mom want to go get her hair and nails done. Andy was in much better shape than his brother because Tina didn't let him eat carbs. Andy also had all of his hair, and I wondered if Tina had a hand in that as well.

The Henderchenkos got there shortly after my mom and I did, and we followed Mak outside to meet them. Mak and Andy hugged and thumped each other on the back. They looked like before-and-after pictures of the same man—the same face and the same height and roughly the same age, but Mak fat and bald and dressed like shit, and Andy thin with hair and wearing a polo shirt and khakis and a belt. If I were my mom I would have been disappointed to find out that I was dating the "before" brother and not the "after" brother, but she didn't seem to mind. Tina was also wearing a polo shirt, with a khaki skirt and wedge sandals. She hugged me and my mom and Mak. Dylan got out of the car dressed like his parents. He didn't look at anyone, and he ducked when Mak tried to tousle his hair. His mom made him say hi and he said it to the ground.

Dylan was twelve and seemed like he was two or three years away from realizing that he hated his parents. For now, though, he liked to sit as close to his mom as possible, and other than that his only hobbies were whining and watching anime. He had this weird energy that clearly came from the shows, like he was playing out the action sequences in his head at all times—cartoon creatures battling in midair, crashing into each other and throwing balls of fire, set to ominous music and slow-motion flashes and explosions.

The Henderchenkos toured the house and confirmed that Dylan would be sleeping with his parents by putting all of their suitcases in the room with the queen bed and the twin bed. Then Tina declared that the women needed to go shopping. Mak had gone to the store, but he had only bought beer, a loaf of bread, a pound of lunch meat, and a box of donuts.

I went with Tina and my mom, and on the way to the store they agreed that the house had been grossly misrepresented on the website, and talked about what the weather was supposed to do all week. My mom was using her polite voice, which she reserves for people in the service industry, my friends' and Noah's friends' moms, and her own mother, from whom she's been estranged for most of her life. I had never wondered if my mom and Tina were friends, but now I understood that they weren't. I was worried that I was going to have to follow them through the store, listening to them talk politely about food, but when we got there they decided to split up.

"Can I take Natalie?" Tina asked my mom. "I haven't seen her in so long." She put her arm around me.

"Sure," said my mom. "I'll meet you guys up front."

Tina started in fruits and vegetables. "So," she said, "how's school?"

"It's fine," I said.

"You're majoring in international relations?"

"I don't know yet," I said. "I don't have to decide until next year."

"The sooner you decide, the better," she said. "You should be looking for internships for next summer."

"Okay," I said.

"I heard you have a boyfriend," she said.

"Sort of," I said. "I'm trying to break up with him."

"Oh no!" she said. "Why?"

"He's very serious about me. Very, very serious."

"But that's a good thing," said Tina.

"Yeah?" I said.

"Yeah," she said.

"Maybe," I said.

"Well I obviously don't know this guy," she said. "But you need to think strategically, Natalie. You need to find a good man in college, because after that all you'll find is bums."

Maybe she was right, but I would rather be single for the rest of my life than be with James.

That night the grown-ups got drunk. Noah went for another "walk" with Petey, and I spent the night reading in bed. Around midnight I went downstairs for a glass of water and found the four of them plastered. Tina told me how much she and Andy loved me and how smart I was and how pretty I was. Mak told me he would love me more if I played golf or really any sport. My mom kissed me good night and sat back down with her arms around Mak.

Early the next morning I woke up to someone starting a racing car. I lay there for a moment trying to block out the noise, but it was too loud. Noah had come home at some point and was fast asleep with pink earplugs in. Petey was awake and looking out the window and wagging his tail. I opened the bedroom door at the same time my mom opened hers. Petey jumped on her.

"I think that's my car," I said.

"No shit," she said.

We went downstairs and out to the porch. Mak had jumper cables between his car and mine, and was trying to start them both.

"Honey!" my mom yelled over the noise. "What the fuck are you doing?"

Mak turned off my car. He looked very hungover or possibly still drunk. He was wearing golf shorts and a wifebeater.

"My car is dead," he said.

"You hear that noise, right?" said my mom.

"Yeah," said Mak.

"You remember that the muffler fell off?"

"Yeah," said Mak.

"Okay. Well. Why don't you take her car and drop it off at the place near the golf course?"

"Fine," said Mak.

"No!" I said. "He's drunk, he'll crash it."

"If he did he would be doing you a favor," said my mom.

Mak transferred his golf bag to the trunk of my car.

"Ugh," I said.

Mak started my car and backed out and drove away. I was pretty sure the whole island was awake now.

"Don't even ask," said my mom.

We went upstairs and back to bed.

When I got back up the women and the boys were eating breakfast. Tina and Dylan Henderchenko were eating fruit, and my mom and my brother were eating Lucky Charms. Dylan had clearly been crying at some point in the last ten minutes.

"What's up?" I said.

"Not a whole lot," said my brother.

I poured myself a bowl of Lucky Charms and sat down.

Dylan started crying. "How come she gets to eat them?" he howled.

My mom looked at me and rolled her eyes. "What's up is Tina and Dylan are going to the amusement park, Noah is going on a hike with Petey, Mak is still golfing, and Andy is going to take a rest day."

A couple of summers ago, my mom started letting Noah take hikes instead of going to the beach. Not coincidentally, that was the year he turned thirteen and started smoking weed. My mom and Mak knew what he was doing, but they didn't care. My mom had been a pothead in high school and Mak still smoked, and they thought it was better than drinking. At first they said he couldn't do it in the house, and on cold nights my brother would put a sweatshirt on Petey, put a parka, a ski mask, and goggles on himself, and they would go for walks. The second winter Noah started smoking in his room, and I didn't know whether he thought nobody noticed or he just didn't care.

"Can I go on the hike with Noah and Petey?" said Dylan.

"No," said Tina.

"Why not?" he said.

"Uh," said Tina and looked at my mom.

"I don't want to go to the amusement park," he said.

He said it so sincerely that I almost felt bad for him.

"Well," said Tina. "I'm sure Noah doesn't want you to tag along."

"I don't mind," said Noah.

"I guess I could go with you guys," said Tina.

"No!" said Dylan. "Noah gets to go by himself!"

"Noah is sixteen," said Tina. "You're twelve."

"I'm almost thirteen," said Dylan.

"You turned twelve last month," said Tina. "Let me think about this."

"It's obviously not my call," said my mom, "but I know Noah would take good care of him and not do anything stupid. Right, honey?"

"Yeah," said Noah.

Dylan lunged at his mom with his hands together, begging.

"I'll talk to your father," said Tina. She turned to my mom. "If the kids go hiking, we could get mani-pedis."

"I would love to, but I just got one," said my mom.

"We could get lunch," said Tina.

"I promised Natalie I would go to the beach with her," said my mom. "Maybe another day?"

· · ·

While Tina and Andy deliberated, Noah went out for a short walk, my mom packed lunches for everyone, and I went upstairs to put on my bathing suit. Dylan watched a show in the living room. Apparently he was usually allowed to watch one show a day, but since it was vacation he was allowed to watch two. I walked through the living room and Dylan screamed at me.

"You made me miss a part!" he said. "Now I have to rewind it and watch it again!"

"Okay," I said. "Sorry."

From what I could tell, he watched a lot more than two shows a day. The night before, I heard him watching on a computer in his room. His parents didn't seem to notice. They thought he was the smartest kid ever. I didn't think he was that smart, but he was probably too smart to be trusted. If he were my kid, I would never have let him out of my sight. Best case, he would watch anime until he had a seizure, worst case, who knows.

Finally Tina came downstairs with a verdict. Dylan could go on the hike with Noah for a maximum of four hours. Every hour, on the hour, he would call Tina to check in. He would take Andy's cell phone. When the four hours were up, the boys would come back to the house. On their way back they could stop at the convenience store to get a snack, but they had to come home to eat it, no loitering.

Dylan was flying around the room, not hearing the instructions. Tina had to sit him down and repeat them.

"I really think they'll be okay." My mom stared at Noah.

"We'll be fine," said Noah.

The boys left for the park, Tina left for town, and my mom and I left for the beach.

"Tina will never speak to me again if Noah gives Dylan weed," said my mom.

"He won't," I said.

"That kid could really use some weed," she said.

"Maybe, but Noah isn't going to give it to him," I said.

We lay on the beach and my mom read and I listened to music. I liked to listen to one song on repeat, and for the past week or so I had been listening to this song from the seventies.

My mom went in the water and then sat on my back. "What're you listening to?"

"This song called 'I've Never Been to Me,'" I said.

"I know that song," she said.

"You do?" I said.

"Yeah, the one about not having kids?"

"No, it's about traveling."

"No, it's about not having kids. The singer regrets all of her sleeping around and traveling around and stuff."

"Are you sure?" I said.

"You're the one listening to it," she said. "Why don't you listen to the lyrics?"

"I am, it's all these names of places."

"Nat, I know that song. It was popular when I was in college. All my girlfriends hated it."

I listened a few more times and decided I still wanted it to be about traveling. I wanted to break up with James and go to any of the faraway places in the song: Monte Carlo, Nice, the Isle of Greece.

I met James my first week of college, and we dated all last year. I stopped liking him a little bit over winter break, when he called every day and I started dreading his calls. When we were at school I didn't mind hanging out with him every day, and every night for that matter. I had sort of had boyfriends in high school, but none who wanted to hang out with me day and night, and none who left me little notes, and none who really, really liked going down on me. I guess there were some red flags, but I didn't know what "red flags" were at the time, and my mom had to tell me what that term meant. The hanging out all the time was probably a red flag, as were the little notes, as was the fact that I would fall asleep while he was going down on me and he would just keep going. Anyway, I didn't get sick of any of that until winter break, and then he wouldn't stop calling, and suddenly I got sick of all of it at the same time.

But when we got back to school he was so nice and I didn't really know anybody else, so I didn't break up with him but I made a lot of rules. We were only allowed to hang out every other day, and we were only allowed to spend the night every other time we hung out. I got the timing for this rule from my bathing rule as a kid—I had to take a bath every other day and wash my hair every other bath. As a kid it seemed like more than enough hair washing, and in college it seemed like more than enough James.

James didn't do well with the rules, so I had to make more rules—no surprising me outside of my classes on the days we weren't supposed to hang out, and then no surprising me even on the days we were supposed to hang out. Then no surprising me with my favorite breakfasts from the dining hall when I was on my way out of my dorm. And then no surprising me at all, for any reason.

Basically, my first year of college was a total bust. I didn't make any friends, and I didn't do well in any of my classes, and I didn't learn anything about life. All I did was date James. And by the end of the year I didn't even want to do that. I told James we could talk on the phone over the summer, but that I was going to be busy and I wasn't going to be able to visit or talk every day or even every other day, due to the being busy. He seemed fine with that and every time we talked he said he couldn't wait to see me in the fall. He also sent me notes and presents, including an Entenmann's coffee cake that I love, overnighted, like they don't have those where I live. After a month of this I couldn't take it anymore, and I came up with the plan of breaking up with him on the way to Emerald Isle in August. Then I waited for weeks and weeks, and here we were, lying on the beach, vacation ruined. I felt better than I had in the car when the muffler first fell off, but this was supposed to be the first week of the rest of my life, when things were going to start getting better.

"I'm gonna go jump in," I said.

"Want me to come with you?" said my mom.

"That's okay," I said. I waded into the cold water and then dove. I swam along the sand for a few minutes and then floated on my back. The water felt good and I felt completely empty, my stomach and my brain, like I didn't have any thoughts at all.

Eventually my mom got in the water and got her head wet, and I followed her back to our towels and lay down. My mom handed me a sandwich and a beer, and we ate our lunch. When I was done I went to sleep, and I woke up under a beach umbrella and next to Mak's big belly.

"You were going to get a real bad burn," he said. "You were out like a drunk. Drooling, the whole nine yards."

"Thanks for the umbrella," I said.

My mom came up from the water and straddled Mak on the chair and shook her hair all over him. He wrapped his arms around her waist and bit her shoulder.

"Get a room," I said.

They ignored me and eventually my mom got off of him and lay down on her towel.

"I took your car in," said Mak.

"I know," I said, "thank you."

"It does not look good," he said.

"What?" I said. "Why not?"

"They said it never would've passed inspection in the state of North Carolina. Bottom is rusted out, holed out, nothing for the muffler to hang on to."

"North Carolina sucks," I said.

"Well if it makes you feel any better, wouldn't have passed inspection in the state of Virginia or the state of anywhere else either."

"We'll work something out, honey," said my mom.

"I'm going to Raleigh no matter what," I said.

"Fine," said my mom.

"I will crawl there if I have to."

"We'll get you there," said my mom.

I checked my phone and had eleven missed calls from Noah. My mom took my phone and called him back. She repeated everything to me and Mak—"Dylan got caught shoplifting . . . a lighter . . . a Zippo . . . Tina is picking them up." We got our stuff together and walked back to the house and waited for them. I was kind of excited. I was pretty sure this was going to be a shit show.

When Tina's car pulled in, both boys and the dog were in the backseat. When they all got out Tina looked furious,

Dylan was crying, Noah looked tired, and Petey looked happy that everybody was together.

"I think we all need to have a conversation," Tina said to my mom.

"Okay," said my mom.

I decided I wasn't included in "we all" and stayed outside with Petey. I watched Noah follow everybody inside and felt bad for him.

I sat under the front windows on the dining room side, where I would be able to hear them. If it had been my mom leading the investigation she would have led everyone to the couches in the living room, but I knew Tina would lead everyone to the table.

"Andy!" I heard Tina yelling. "We're here! Come down!"

"Tina," Andy said, already downstairs. "Please, don't yell."

"Somebody has to yell," she said.

"Okay," he said. A chair dragged on the floor.

"Dylan, do you want to tell us what happened?" said Tina.

"It's not my fault," Dylan sobbed.

"What happened?" said Andy.

Dylan cried harder. "Noah took things!" he said.

"Is that true?" said my mom.

"No," said Noah. "Well, I took matches."

"You did?" said Tina.

"Matches are free," said my mom.

"But not for kids," said Tina.

"It's not shoplifting," said my mom.

"Why would anyone take matches in front of a little kid?" said Tina.

"I'm not a little kid!" said Dylan.

"I didn't even think about it," said Noah. "I always put some in my pocket."

"How is Dylan supposed to know the difference between matches and a lighter?" said Tina. "Dylan, did you know that you weren't supposed to take the lighter?"

"No," he wailed. "I didn't know!"

I kept waiting for one of the men to say something. An elderly couple walked by very slowly. The woman was holding the man's arm and it looked like the man couldn't see very well or at all. Petey wagged his tail and I waved, and the woman waved back.

"It seems like everyone did something wrong here," said Tina through the window. "We shouldn't have let them go out on their own. Noah shouldn't have taken the matches. Dylan shouldn't have taken the lighter. Andy?"

"Hold on," said my mom. "Noah taking the matches didn't mean Dylan had to take the lighter."

"Dylan was clearly influenced by Noah's actions," said Tina. "Andy!"

"I agree," said Andy.

"Noah didn't do anything wrong," said my mom.

"He shouldn't be taking matches," said Tina.

"That's not your problem," said Mak.

"It's my problem now," said Tina. "Isn't it?"

"No, it's not," said Mak. "Dylan is your problem, Noah is our problem."

"Noah's not a problem," said my mom.

"You know what I mean," said Mak.

"Well, Dylan's never been a problem before today," said Tina.

Someone snorted.

"Fuck you, Mak," said Andy.

"Okay, boys, you can be excused," said Tina. "Dylan, go to our room and wait for us to come up."

Noah must have made a gesture, because my mom said, "Yeah, honey."

I heard Dylan and Noah go up the creaky stairs, and then heard one of them come back down. Noah came outside and I crawled out from under the window. He pointed to the road with his thumb, and Petey and I followed him. We could hear the grown-ups raising their voices as we walked away.

"You hear all that?" he said.

"Yeah," I said. "I hate that kid."

"He's okay," said Noah. "It's not his fault."

"It's not his fault that he sucks?"

Noah laughed. "Yeah."

"You really think he didn't know not to take it?"

"Oh he knew," said Noah. "He came running out with this crazy look on his face, and then when he realized the guy was behind him he tried to make a run for it."

"Oh shit."

"Yeah."

"Why didn't you tell them that?"

"Wouldn't have helped," he said.

When we got to the park Petey ran ahead, wagging his whole body. Noah lit his joint. He passed it to me and I took a hit. I almost never smoked anymore and it caught me in the throat. Noah laughed.

"Mom and Mak stood up for you," I said.

"Yeah," he said.

The second hit wasn't as bad, and by the end of the joint I was used to it again. Maybe I would have been happier if I smoked more weed. Everything slowed down in a way that was very relaxing. In high school Noah would sometimes talk me into smoking with him at night, or on the way to school in the morning. Whenever we smoked before my precalculus class, I felt smart. I still wouldn't know what the numbers meant, but the board would seem organized, and the numbers would seem independent from each other, like they were each doing their own job. On those mornings I wondered if I was going to solve some problem that nobody else had ever solved in the whole history of math.

. . .

When we got back the sun was setting. My mom and Mak met us in the yard and said we were going out for pizza. Mak got in the driver's seat and we all got in the car.

"I'm really sorry," said Noah.

"It's okay, honey," said my mom. She reached back and patted him on the leg. "It's not about you."

At the pizza place no one knew what to say, so Mak gave my mom, and by default us, a play-by-play of his game that morning. Usually my mom shut him down as soon as he started talking about golf, but tonight she was asking questions and nodding.

On the way back to the house, my mom turned around to face us. "I was thinking maybe we should head out tomorrow," she said. "Nat, we could pick up your car and stop at James's on the way home."

"We've only been here for one day," I said.

"I thought you were dying to break up with him," said my mom.

"I am," I said. "But you guys don't have to come."

"I want to," said my mom. "I'll feel more comfortable being in the car with you, if something goes wrong. And I think Noah is ready to go."

"I am," said Noah.

"What about Mak?" I said.

"I'll stay," said Mak. "Keep up appearances."

"And play golf," said my mom.

"That's another consideration," said Mak.

I texted James to say I was going to stop by the next day.

Back at the house, the Henderchenkos were in their bedroom. We went to bed quietly.

I woke up to Noah squeezing my wrist.

"I'm going to go watch the sunrise," he said.

"What?" I said.

"You should watch it with me," he said. "It will make you feel better."

I made myself wake up and we took our blankets and pillows off our beds and walked to the beach. We lay down on one blanket and put the other one over us. Petey lay down on top, with his butt on me and his head on Noah.

Soon there was the faintest glow at the end of the water. I propped myself up on my elbows. The sun came up slowly and then quickly. And Noah was right, it did make me feel a little bit better.

We watched until the sun took its place in the sky.

When we got back to the house, Mak was putting his golf clubs in his trunk.

"What are you two doing now?" Mak said.

"We watched the sunrise," I said.

"Deep," said Mak. "How'd you wake up in time?"

"I didn't go to sleep," said Noah.

"You didn't?" I said.

"Genius," said Mak. "Listen, y'all want to get some breakfast? We can get donuts and I'll take you to get your car, Nat."

I got in the passenger seat and Noah and Petey got in the backseat. Noah went to sleep immediately. He couldn't get up when we got to the donut place so we got him his two favorites and put the bag on the floor in front of him. When Mak and I were done with our donuts, he said we had some time to kill until the car place opened, and that it was the perfect amount of time for a round of pitch and putt. I wanted to resist but it was too early in the morning.

When we got there we took Petey with us and left Noah in the car. The course was thick with fog. On my first hit I almost made it to the green.

"Not bad, Fat Nat," said Mak.

My mom didn't let him call me that, but I didn't mind because I wasn't fat and he was. On my next hit I almost made it to the hole. Mak told me to sink it in, so I did.

"Par!" he yelled.

I pretended like I didn't care, but my heart leapt. I wondered if it was possible that I was suddenly good at golf.

On the way to the next hole I asked Mak if we ruined the vacation.

"No," he said. "Not for me, anyway."

When we got to the next hole I missed the ball twice and then hit it about fifteen feet.

"Ooh," said Mak.

It took me like nine hits to get the ball up onto the green.

"Thanks for sticking up for Noah," I said.

"He didn't steal anything," said Mak.

On my twelfth or thirteenth hit I got the ball in the hole.

"Honestly, that kid's a little piece of shit," said Mak. "I mean, he's my nephew, I love him. Doesn't mean I wouldn't trade him for another one if I could."

"Mak!"

"What?"

At the next hole Mak told me to hit down on the ball, but I missed and hit the ground so hard it sent vibrations to my brain, and made Petey jump.

"Christ, Nat," said Mak.

"Sorry," I said.

"So, this boyfriend of yours," he said while I swung again.

"Soon to be ex-boyfriend," I said.

"Right," he said.

"I feel bad," I said. "He didn't do anything wrong."

"Yes he did," said Mak. "He was boring as hell."

"Shit, Mak," I said. "Thanks for telling me now."

"What?" he said. "You gotta learn these things. You gotta learn them the hard way, otherwise you don't learn them at all."

I hit my ball halfway down the fairway and he hit his to the green.

"You need a man who knows how to deal with you."

"What's that supposed to mean?" I said.

"You and your mom," he said, "you two are real fire-crackers. You need men who know how to set you off."

"Why would I want to be set off?" I said.

"Because if you're not you're bored out of your mind."

"I don't know," I said.

We played the rest of the holes almost in silence, except for Mak trying to give me pointers on my game.

When we finished the ninth hole he said, "You're getting real good."

"Really?" I said.

"No, not really," he said.

Noah was fast asleep in the backseat, but there was icing on his mouth. Petey licked him and he stirred. We drove to the car place.

"I got 'er up and running," said the car guy.

"Will she make it to Virginia?" said Mak.

"Maybe," said the guy, "but not more. Never would've passed inspection in the state of North Carolina."

"I heard," I said.

"The bottom of the car is rusted out. You got a hole in the back where the muffler was, and pretty soon you're gonna have some holes in the cab. This floor is gonna crumble."

"Is that safe?" said Mak.

"No, sir," said the mechanic. "Car has a floor for a reason."

The car seemed fine to me. Mak followed me back to the house. When we got there my mom had packed up our stuff, and we loaded it into the car and transferred Noah and Petey to my backseat. Tina came out to say good-bye to me and my mom. She said she didn't want to wake up Andy and Dylan, but that they said bye. She gave us both hugs, like she wasn't having a huge fight with my mom.

When we crossed the bridge I asked my mom if we were ever going back.

"We'll see," she said.

My mom and Noah slept most of the way to Raleigh, but when we got close my mom woke up and asked me if I was nervous.

"I guess," I said.

"I'm proud of you," she said.

"Why?" I said.

"Because it's easy to stay in a relationship that's not bad but not good," she said.

I wondered what relationship she was thinking of. Obviously not her and Mak, which was gross but definitely good. Maybe she meant her and my dad. Or Tina and Andy.

"Like Tina and Andy?" I said.

"Ha!" said my mom. "Oh god, sweetie, you couldn't end up like Tina and Andy if you tried."

We stopped at a mall in Raleigh and woke Noah up. My mom went inside and Noah and Petey disappeared into the trees on the other side of the parking lot.

I drove up the highway feeling jittery. I couldn't wait to get there, but I had no idea what would happen when I did. I tried to imagine some best-case scenarios. Maybe he had another girlfriend already. Maybe she liked surprises, but he didn't even need to surprise her because they were always together. Maybe James sent me the coffee cake out of cheater guilt.

Or maybe he would come out to me. For this scenario I ignored his great love of the female body, and concentrated on his sensitivity and his strong commitment to feminism. If he was gay he would want to stay friends, but I thought it might be too late for that. I was so sick of him.

I tried not to let myself think about one other scenario, but it had occurred to me at some point in the last few weeks, and had been creeping into my thoughts ever since. I didn't want James to die, but if I got to his house and he had been in a terrible accident, or had succumbed to a brief but devastating illness, I would be off the hook. Not only would I be off the hook, I would be like a girlfriend-widow.

When I got there, James's parents were in the driveway and they gave me hugs and got into their van and drove away. I wondered how they knew what I was about to do.

James looked happy to see me. He also looked monogamous, straight, and alive. He gave me a big hug and a kiss and he went back in to get the lemonade he had made from scratch. I sat down on the wicker couch on the porch.

"I'm so happy to see you," he said when he came back. He sat next to me.

"Uh," I said.

His face fell a little.

"We need to talk."

His face fell the rest of the way.

"I don't think I want to be together anymore," I said. "I'm sorry."

"What happened?" he said. "What changed?"

"Nothing changed," I said. "I just want something else."

"There's someone else?" he said.

"No, I want something else. From my life."

"What else do you want?" he said.

"I don't know," I said. "But don't you want something else too? Something different?"

"No," he said.

"I think this will be better for you," I said. "You'll find a better girlfriend."

"No I won't."

We sat there for a minute that felt like a year. Finally the effort of keeping my eyes open made one of them water.

James looked at me and then put his arm around me and tried to guide my head to his shoulder. I realized he thought I was crying so I put my head down, even though that was the number one last thing I wanted to do. He wrapped his arms around me, and we sat like that forever.

Finally he let go and said, "We don't have to make a decision right now."

"But I already made a decision." That sounded bad so I added, "I'm really sad about it, though."

Now he put his head on my shoulder and started to cry. I patted him on the leg. Soon, but not soon enough, his parents came back, saw him crying, gave me a look of death, and went inside.

"I guess your parents hate me now," I said.

"No they don't," he said. "I will never hate you."

"Okay," I said. "I guess I should get back on the road."

James walked me to my car and gave me a very long hug that involved swaying from side to side. When he let me go I got in the car, and I felt something give under my right foot. I shut the door and looked under the mat, where there was now a hole that I could see his driveway through.

I thought I would have more time before the floor crumbled. I rolled down the window.

"Is your car okay?" he said.

"Yup," I said, "great."

"I'll see you in September," he said.

"Yup," I said, hoping that he wouldn't. "I'm sorry again."

He didn't say anything. I backed out and was about to pull away when he yelled, "Wait!" He pointed to a spot on the blacktop. "Did that just fall off your car?"

"Nope," I yelled. "I don't think so." I waved and pulled away.

Driving back to the mall I thought I would feel electrified or something, but instead I felt calm. When I got there, I pulled into the parking lot and called my mom and Noah. My mom came out of the mall.

"Mission accomplished?" she said.

"Mission accomplished," I said.

Noah and Petey came out of the trees and got in.

We headed toward Charlottesville. The sound of the road tore through the hole in the floor and filled up the car.

DESERT HEARTS

When I moved to San Francisco with my fiancé, he started practicing law and I started selling toys. I was supposed to start practicing law too, but I didn't have the heart. I almost didn't even have the heart to take the bar, but I found it when my dad threatened to cut me off. And then he cut me off right afterward anyway, because he said it was time to get a job, and if I didn't want either of the jobs he had found for me, I was on my goddamn own.

I did apply to two law firms in San Francisco but I got rejected from both of them. Actually, rejected would mean they considered me, which there was no evidence of them doing. So now my job search strategy was to look for Help

Wanted signs in windows, which would have given my dad an aneurysm, and which concerned my fiancé. Danny gently suggested that I stay home until I could think of something I actually wanted to do and apply for it. But I couldn't think of anything I actually wanted to do.

I applied to some restaurants and some stores, but they all wanted someone with experience. And I didn't have any experience except working at my dad's firm in high school, another, bigger firm in college, and another, bigger firm in law school. My dad's firm and the last firm were the two that had made me offers, but they were both in Los Angeles and Danny's offer was in San Francisco, and since I didn't care at all and Danny cared a lot, we went to San Francisco.

I tried to look for small stores that didn't require folding T-shirts or any other special skills, and that looked like they might not have a lot of customers. One day I went out and applied to two movie stores in our neighborhood, where both of the managers were teenagers. Then I applied to a bagel store where all I would have to do was work the register. No putting cream cheese on bagels, because I needed training for that. Then I rode my bike to Dolores Park and walked around. Near the park I saw a Help Wanted sign in the window of an adult toy store called Desert Hearts. I went in thinking I would look around and then talk to someone, but the store was about ten feet by fifteen feet, and there was only one person there, so I had to talk to her right away. She was maybe sixty and she had short hair and a rat tail.

"Hi, can I help you?" she said.

"I was wondering if you guys are still hiring," I said.

"Oh," she said. "Yes we are. Are you, uh, lesbian?"

I looked around and took note of the wall of dildos.

"Yeah," I said, "I am." I gave her my biggest smile.

"Oh," she said, "great. Well, I'm just filling in here, but I know they're looking for someone full-time. The manager works at our store in the Castro. Ask for Chad."

"Thanks so much," I said. "I'm Brenda."

"Nice to meet you. I'm Eunice." She smiled and we shook hands. I realized my engagement ring was on my other hand and hoped Eunice hadn't noticed. She gave me a business card and I left.

I looked up directions to the store, Making Love, and rode back through the park to the Castro. When I got there I put my ring in my pocket, and went in and asked for Chad. Chad was huge and black and he was wearing a T-shirt that barely fit around his arms. I was pretty sure I could see every muscle underneath.

"Oh, great!" he said when I told him I wanted to apply to work at Desert Hearts. "That's great!"

He took me into the back and asked me a million questions about my employment history, my sexual history, and what I was doing in the hilly city. I told him I moved with my girlfriend Nadeen, who was a lawyer, and that I'd been a sexual health educator in college. The man at the bagel store had seemed concerned that I graduated from law school, so I decided to leave that part out. The sexual health educator part was true. And Nadeen was not completely untrue. I slept with her my freshman year of college after my dad told me that he didn't want to hear about any of this "gay until graduation" stuff if I insisted on attending a girls' school.

Then Chad told me about the stores, talking a mile a minute, and soon we were out on the floor and he was showing me the lesbian section and the exclusive harness they carried and the line of dildos they sold to go with it. The harness was really special because it was made out of leather and the ring was internal. Chad let me hold the harness and feel the ring, which apparently was around the hole underneath the two layers of leather. I didn't ask what the ring was for or why internal was better.

"Wow, this is nice," I said.

"I know, right?" said Chad. "I mean I don't know, but, you know."

"Ha," I said, "right."

There were a million dildos in a million colors, in sizes from baby carrot to miniature log.

Chad introduced me to the people working at Making

Love, and said I would be working at Desert Hearts by myself, and if I could work five days a week, one of the Love girls would fill in on the other two days. Eunice was a friend of the owner, Pamela, and was just filling in until they found someone more permanent.

"And I would like that to be you!" said Chad. "I have to run this by Pamela, but I know she will think you are just adorable!"

"Great," I said.

When I got home I took a shower and made stuffed peppers and waited for Danny for a while, then ate the peppers by myself and watched a two-hour dating show. My dad called to bother me so I told him I was going to work at a sex toy store and he said he didn't have time for my jokes, and to call him back when I was ready to get serious about my life.

When Danny got home at ten I told him I might have gotten a job.

"Where?" he said.

"At this store in the Mission," I said. "A sex toy store."

"Ha," he said.

"No really," I said.

"Really?" he said, looking worried.

"I can still look for law jobs," I said, to make him feel

better. "But this way I can make some money and have some interim work to put on my resume."

"I don't think you can put that on your resume," he said. "Do you even know anything about sex toys?"

"Yes," I said. "As a matter of fact, I do. I learned a lot today. And I have that vibrator."

"That blue dolphin thing?" he said. "Has that ever had batteries in it?"

"So?" I said.

"Okay," he said. "Well, I hope you get the job if you want it."

"Thanks baby," I said. "I want it."

I guess thinking about the toys made Danny feel sexy, because he got me started when we got into bed, and we had sex for the second time in San Francisco. The first time we were exhausted from moving, and giddy because we had had too many beers to celebrate. Then when Danny started working and it didn't happen again, I started worrying that it was the beginning of the end, and in twenty years when our kids claimed we only had sex twice, once for each of them, it would be more or less true.

But that night after Desert Hearts and Eunice and Chad, it was as good as it had ever been. I choked myself up thinking how grateful I was to have someone who knew my body by heart and could get me off in two minutes or two hours, and especially how grateful I was when it was two hours. When we finally went to sleep, I had a dream that I worked at the store and I had to wear a tiny dildo necklace.

The next afternoon Chad called to say I got the job, and he wanted to know if I could work the next day. The next day was Saturday but I said okay. He asked me if I thought I remembered enough from Making Love to come up with some talking points for the harness and the dildo collection. I said yes and had a feeling that I was going to spend the next twenty-four hours reading about lesbian sex and sex toys on the internet. He said he would meet me at Desert Hearts at noon to train me to use the register and some other store-specific stuff, like the sex machine.

"Great," I said.

When Danny got home I told him I got the job and was going to start tomorrow. He said it was fine; he had a lot of work to do anyway.

"And maybe I'll come visit you," he said.

"Oh god," I said. "Please don't."

Later he caught me printing out pictures from the dildo website, which I was planning to use for flash cards to help me learn the names of the different models. He laughed at me and I laughed too. He kissed my neck and I felt the hairs there stand up. I followed him to the back of the apartment, hopeful, but by the time I finished brushing my teeth he was asleep.

. . .

On Saturday I rode to Desert Hearts and Chad tried to teach me how to use the register, which was a computer with the most complex software I had ever used. I was finally able to make a successful transaction around two in the afternoon, and Chad sighed a big sigh of relief and brought in some books from his car, put them on the table at the front of the store, and told me he was leaving.

Two women who had been whispering in the dildo section asked me for help. They had picked out a fabric harness and were trying to decide on a dildo, and wanted to know what other colors "Buck" came in. I told them he came in three skin tones, vanilla, caramel, and chocolate. And I asked them if they had seen our exclusive harness and gave them the whole speech about the virtually seamless leather and the internal ring and everything. I didn't think they would go for it since it cost twice as much as the one they picked out, but they did. They said they were glad they talked to me because they weren't thinking of it as an investment before. When I turned around Chad was still there, folding shirts. The women picked the caramel Buck, and I checked them out with no problems.

When they were gone Chad said, "See, you are smart! That was just great! You're going to do great. The only thing is don't call the dildos 'he,' okay? Most lesbians don't really like that."

"Oops," I said, "okay." That made sense but it really seemed like a stretch to imagine Buck as female or sexless. Buck had a very realistic-looking head, and veins up and down the shaft. Buck didn't have balls, but several of the other dildos in that collection did. And Buck was circumcised, but some of the others weren't. I could see calling the dildos in the other, smoother, more abstract collections "she," but when I see a head, veins, and wrinkled balls, I think "he." I wondered who was designing these things and why they thought lesbians wanted penis replicas.

Chad left and later called to see if I could work the next day so that I could meet Pamela and have her show me around.

Before Pamela came in I saw her parking her motorcycle in front of the store and taking her helmet off. She looked like Eunice, but heavier and without the rat tail, and when she came in I couldn't tell if she had a really kind face or a tired face. She gave me a once-over and a terse smile and I decided on tired face.

"I'm Pam," she said. "Thanks for working on such short notice."

She explained everything to me again, looking at me skeptically the whole time. In the middle of the harness speech she looked at me and said, "Have you ever actually used a harness?"

"Yes," I said. "Of course. I've used yours. I mean the Desert Hearts one. My girlfriend and I got it when we were up here last year."

"Oh really?" said Pam. She looked pleased but didn't smile. "Do you like it?"

"Yeah we love it," I said. "I've never worn anything more comfortable."

"Huh," she said. "Great."

Maybe I shouldn't have said I was the one who wore it. I guess if I was a lesbian I wouldn't be a top. But I figured I would be willing to at least try it.

I listened through the harness speech and the dildo speech and the lube speech, and by the time we got to the vibrators I started to get impatient and started cutting her off. Like when she said, "The Eroscillator is the number-one-rated stimulator," I said, "It was engineered in Switzerland and university-tested in the U.S. There is no better vibrator."

"Good," she said. "I guess Chad went over everything."

When Pam got back on her motorcycle and rode away, I tried out all of the vibrators on my nose like she told me to tell the customers to do, but I wasn't sure that gave me a good sense of how they would feel on my clit. I did like the Eroscillator though. There were seven attachments and I cleaned off the Grapes and Cockscomb attachment with a Clorox wipe and massaged my face with it. At the end of the day, I bought the Eroscillator with my employee discount. Danny laughed about it at first, but then we had sex and we used it, and it made him feel good and it made me feel like I was on another planet.

The next morning Chad called and asked if I could work at Making Love instead, and when I got there he told me that Pam was concerned about me working at Desert Hearts. He held his hands up like, *What can you do?* and started explaining all of the men's color-coded leather accessories.

The other people working were Marc and Estelle, and they worked the floor while I stayed at the register. Some guys came in and asked for poppers and I looked in the cock ring display case, wondering what might be called poppers. Marc was in the video section, and I didn't want to ask him what they were, so I just asked him where they were.

"Um, they are NOWHERE," he yelled back, "because we do not have POPPERS, because they're ILLEGAL!"

"Oh," I said, and tried to smile at the guys as they high-tailed it out of the store.

Marc told me that poppers were muscle relaxants and he also told me that Pam didn't want me to work at Desert Hearts because I didn't look gay.

"That's discrimination," I said.

"What are you going to do, call a lawyer?" said Marc.

"Maybe," I said.

"She didn't really fire you."

"True."

I worked at Making Love all that week and Eunice worked at Desert Hearts until they found a replacement, Carol, who had a crew cut. Marc said if I was really mad he would cut my hair and lend me some cargo shorts. It was clear to me that I needed a rat tail, and later Danny told me he would pay me a hundred dollars to get a mullet, but Marc thought I needed something more subtle, like a faux hawk.

But then on her third day, Carol the real lesbian dropped the entire computer on the floor by accident. Somehow Pam didn't fire her for that, but Carol never showed up to work again. Marc told me that Pam begged Eunice to come back before she decided I would have to work at Desert Hearts again. I was almost sad to leave Making Love because I liked working with everyone there and I liked gay men—when it came to sex toys, they were much more outgoing than lesbians—but I was glad to be by myself and read all of the books, and the new cash register was so easy. I just typed in the prices, and if something wasn't marked, I made up a price that I thought sounded fair.

I asked Chad if he could start sending someone from Making Love to work some of the shifts, like he had originally promised. He did, and I got Sundays off. On those mornings, Danny and I slept in and went and got eggs Benedict and talked about whether we should get a Newfoundland or a mutt. I wanted a little tiny dog that would sit in my lap all the time. I imagined bringing her to the store. I imagined that I owned it and instead of sex toys it sold something else, like maybe cheese, or actually maybe dog toys. Danny wanted a Newfoundland because his family always had Newfoundlands. Those dogs don't live for very long so his family had had a lot of them, and they were all named Boomer—Boomer the first, Boomer the second, et cetera. Danny could somehow tell them apart, and he choked up at the thought of each one.

Now that I was back at Desert Hearts, I realized how different the stores were. At Making Love, the boy toys were front and center—butt toys, cock rings, and what I was sure was more lube than even the city of San Francisco could use. The backdrop was leather accessories, bondage accessories, a sex swing, porn, and in one corner, the lesbian and straight stuff, just in case.

At Desert Hearts, the space was so small that everything was kind of front and center, but it was the books you saw first. Sometimes people looked at them if they were too nervous to head right for the good stuff, which must have been the books' purpose, but no one ever bought them.

I obviously didn't know what lesbians wanted, but I

didn't think we needed the books to make it a classy place. I thought we should send a more affirming message like, *You don't have to pretend to look at these books*. If it were up to me, I would have had one shelf around the store, vibrators on one long wall, harnesses on the short wall, and then dildos on the other long wall, and maybe lube by the register. Very minimal and chic. Kind of like a nice jewelry store, but with softer lighting.

I think I would have done without the sex machine. It was basically a motorized dick and when you plugged it in, the dick flew in and out of the console. It was four hundred dollars and it took up a lot of space on a shelf at the back of the store. On Friday nights drunk women would come in and ask me to turn it on. There was one group that came in almost every week. It was four or five women and they always looked like they had been drinking since noon, and they almost always got out of hand and I had to kick them out. I thought one of them liked me. Her name was Lucy and she hung out by the cash register and didn't ask questions about any of the merchandise, which I thought was smart. She was my age and pretty and I probably flirted with her more than I should have, but I was bored.

One week she was distracting me, talking about how she could show me around the city if I wanted. She was saying we should go to this restaurant called Carmen's, if I like Cuban food, which I do, when I looked up and saw the loudest woman, a tiny blonde with a pixie cut and huge boobs, on top of the shelf and on top of the machine, pretending to use it. The other women were laughing hysterically.

"Okay," I said. "Time to go."

She didn't get down and I had to go over and pull her off the shelf with Lucy's help.

"I want it so bad!" the little blonde said as she was getting down.

All her friends laughed again but I didn't think she was kidding.

The next time Pam came in to bring more custom harnesses, she quizzed me about what lesbian bars I liked to go to. I wasn't ready, so I told her Nadeen worked too much and we didn't go out.

"You've never gone out to a bar," she said.

I tried to think if I had heard of any. "No," I said. "Not yet." I asked her what bars she recommended for our next free night and she squinted at me and said she didn't know but she thought maybe the younger women went out in Bernal Heights.

"Thanks," I said.

I didn't know if Nadeen worked too much, but Danny did. He stayed late almost every weeknight and went in for full days on the weekends. I tried to be cool like I was when we were in school, when he would disappear for weeks at a time and then come back to me only to pass out cold for another week.

One morning I woke up and Danny hadn't come home, and as I was leaving for work he came in. He looked like the old Danny, two bruised eyes and a shadow beard.

"I am so sorry," he said.

"Oh baby," I said. I hugged him and kissed him on his eyes. "Can you go to sleep now?"

"No," he said, "I just need to take a shower and change my clothes."

"Shit," I said. "Want me to take a shower with you?"

"Not now, babe. I'm sorry."

He got in the shower and I made toast for him and left.

The less Danny slept, the more I did. I started getting into bed when I got home and sleeping twelve or fourteen hours until I had to go to work again.

My dad kept calling to harass me. He thought I was lying about the store. On one call I told him it was a lesbian sex toy store, and on another call I gave him the name and the address and told him to look it up if he didn't believe me. On another call I offered to send him a pay stub. On another call I told him I was trying to get pregnant. I knew I shouldn't antagonize him, but I couldn't help it. He seemed so far away, now that I was in San Francisco and he was in Los Angeles, and now that my bank account was no longer attached to his.

It wasn't a total lie that I wanted to get pregnant. Danny and I were planning to work for a year or two, get married, and then have kids. But I was becoming more and more convinced that sooner would be better than later, so that I could have some company.

I also couldn't stop thinking about sex, which I guess was inevitable. I wanted to have it more than ever, and I was having it less than ever. I started using the toys by myself. I had never even really masturbated before, but now I did it almost every day. I mostly used the Eroscillator and a gold glitter dildo, which had a retracted foreskin but no veins or balls. I also purchased another vibrator called a Rock-Chick, which was U-shaped and which you were supposed to rock in and out. I hadn't been able to get the hang of it, which was what Pam told me to tell customers, that they just needed to get the hang of it. Now I knew that was a lie. Something was anatomically incorrect. So I gave myself a refund, and I marked them down from $39.99 to $19.99. Pam was very excited when I called Chad and told him we were out. But she didn't restock them, which confirmed she knew they were no fun. We also sold out of some 99-cent bullet vibrators, which I had marked down from $4.99 when I realized that all of their batteries had leaked acid.

In my sex toy stupor I also bought a butt plug for Danny, although I was doubtful that he would want to try it, or that we would ever be home at the same time again. It was black-and-blue marbled silicone, very masculine, and I was prepared with a speech that Chad gave me when I worked at Making Love about how straight men have prostates too.

One day I was cleaning the store and trying to decide what toy I wanted to try next when I heard Pam's bike outside. My heart started beating faster, but then I remembered I was cleaning and I was wearing a work shirt and both of those things were good. I wiped down the next shelf and put the pocket vibrators back, and saw Pam looking through the window. I waved and she came in.

"Hi Pam," I said.

"Hi Brenda," she said. "How's it going?"

"Oh good," I said. "Just cleaning."

"Great," said Pam. "I just wanted to tell you that we're having a little birthday party for Chad at Making Love on Friday night. Bring your girlfriend."

Since it was a command I said, "Okay."

"What's her name again?" said Pam.

"Nadeen."

"What does she look like?"

"She's gorgeous," I said, remembering seeing Nadeen

around campus and in the dark in her twin bed. "She's half black and half Native American."

"You know, you don't look gay at all."

"Really?" I said.

"No," she said.

"I guess I've always been pretty feminine," I said. "Although I have always wanted to cut my hair."

"Really," said Pam.

"Yeah," I said. "I won't give you my whole sob story about my dad, but now that he's not supporting me anymore I feel like I can finally do it." I was starting to feel like I was telling the truth.

"It's liberating." Pam smiled at me for the second time since I met her. "It really is."

By Friday I still hadn't come up with a plan. I searched Facebook for any friends of friends who lived in the Bay Area and looked like they might be half black and half Native American, and planned to offer them money or an Eroscillator, but I couldn't come up with anyone. My next best idea was to bring the cash deposit to Making Love, tell Pam that I couldn't stay because Nadeen was in the hospital with a ruptured spleen, and then start crying. I wondered if it was suspicious that "spleen" rhymed with "Nadeen."

On the way to work on Friday I got a haircut. It was sort of an impulse decision. I rode by the hair salon every day, but never thought anything of it. Now, faced with losing my job due to my inability to produce a girlfriend, I stopped and went in and asked a punky-looking girl to cut it all off. I didn't know why I cared if I lost my job, but I did.

"You sure about this?" said the girl.

"Yes," I said. "I need to look gayer."

"Okay," she said.

"Can you do one thing?" I said. "Can you cut the front first and can we take a picture?"

"Fine."

She started cutting from the top of my head and I watched the pieces fall to the floor. She cut quickly, breathing like she was sleeping.

She gave me a perfect mullet. The back was so gross and long. She took pictures from a few different angles and gave me back my phone. It was like I was looking at pictures of someone else. I sent Danny the best one with a message that said, "You owe me $100."

I watched in the mirror as she cut the back.

"Can you make it shorter?" I asked.

"No," she said.

"I'm freaking out," I said.

"Close your eyes," she said.

Soon the rest of the hair was off of my neck, and my head felt very light.

I opened my eyes but she told me to close them again.

She put something that smelled good in my hair and told me I could open. My hair was longer than I had wanted— to the bottom of my ears with sort of side-swept bangs. But I looked like a new woman, and that was exactly what I had wanted.

"Do I look gay?" I said.

"You look gayer," she said.

I was practicing my look of panic for when I told Pam about Nadeen's spleen when Lucy and her drunk friends came in to play with the sex machine.

"Can you show us how that machine works?" said the little blonde.

"Whoa," said Lucy. "You look great."

"Thanks," I said. I went to go plug in the machine.

"I'm sorry that this is, like, a routine," Lucy said when I sat back down behind the register. "Wow, you look really good."

"Thanks," I said.

"I don't really mind stopping by here," she said, biting her lip.

I wanted to look at the ceiling and pretend I hadn't heard her, but I forced myself to look her in the eye and smile. "Listen, what are you doing later?"

Her eyes got bigger. "Nothing," she said. "Going dancing with these winners."

"Would you want to come to a birthday party with me? It's at our other store, in the Castro."

Now she was beaming. "I would love to," she said.

"Okay," I said. I couldn't think of anything else to say, and nobody was doing anything bad to the sex machine, so I couldn't kick the women out. Mercifully, Lucy rounded up her friends and gave me the sweetest smile on the way out.

"I'll meet you here at ten," she said.

I tried to decide if there was anything else I wanted to buy before I got fired. I had most of the things that might have been useful to me, but I rang up a couple of bottles of lube for when I used my dildo, or for when I hit menopause in twenty-five years.

Lucy showed up at ten of ten, alone and smiling. My heart sped up a little. I put the money in the deposit bag and moved my bike to the storage room. We got a cab, and on the way to the Castro I asked Lucy questions and when she tried to ask me anything I cut her off with more questions. She was a nutritionist who specialized in HIV/AIDS care. She lived alone, except for her dog and her four cats, in the Sunset. She wasn't a hoarder, people just kept dumping cats on her. One of the cats had feline HIV and she thought it was funny but not really funny that she had to develop a special diet and cook for him. She was from

Texas, her parents were Catholic but they loved her anyway, she'd gone to another of the Seven Sisters. She said all of her gay friends were either married to each other or not gay anymore, and I said most of mine weren't gay anymore.

When we got to Making Love she smiled at me and we went in. It was mostly Chad's friends, who were his boyfriend, an old white guy, and a lot of similar couples— gorgeous, sinewy men of color and their older, rubberier, whiter boyfriends. Marc was standing in front of the register, pouring himself some champagne. "What the fuck!" he said, and gave me two kisses.

"This is Lucy," I said. "This is Marc."

They said hi.

I saw Pam staring at me from the video section and realized that my plan might work.

"I'll be right back," I told Lucy.

"Wow," said Pam when I got to her. "You did it."

"Yup," I said.

"Okay, well," she said. "Anyway. That's not your girl-friend."

I tried to look guilty. "No, it's not," I said. "She had to work late, again, like every night, so. This is like the thou-sandth time she's canceled on me. I'm never dating a cor-porate lawyer again."

"So who is that?"

"That's Lucy."

"I see," said Pam, and smiled at me for the third time

ever. "Be careful. Everybody finds out everything around here."

"Okay," I said.

I went back to Lucy, who was looking at or past the case with the cock rings.

"Hey, sorry. My boss. I'm kind of scared of her."

She smiled. "No worries."

I poured myself a glass of champagne.

"So," said Lucy, "what about you? Where are you from?"

"I wasn't done questioning you!" I said. "So, where are you from?"

Lucy laughed. "I already told you, the Lone Star State."

"Oh right," I said. "Where did you meet your friends?"

"At work, actually," she said.

"Really," I said.

She laughed. "Yeah, they're different there. They keep it pretty professional."

Estelle came up behind Lucy.

"Hey," I said. "This is my friend Lucy."

"Hello," said Estelle. "Brenda, Marc would like to see you in his office."

"His office?" I looked around and saw Marc sitting in the sex swing at the back of the store.

"Oh Jesus," I said. Estelle laughed her deep laugh.

I looked at Lucy. "I'm fine," she said.

I went back to Marc. "Yes?" I said.

"What the fuck is that?"

"A haircut."

"I told you to get a faux hawk."

"Maybe next time," I said.

"But what the fuck is that?" He gestured toward Lucy.

"Nothing."

"Where did you get her?"

"I can't tell you."

"Please tell me you didn't get her from the store." He stared at me. "Oh my god, Brenda!"

"What? I don't know anyone else."

"I could have set you up with a loaner."

"Shh," I said. "Can we talk about this later? Or never?"

"Oh, we will definitely be talking about it later."

Chad had his shirt off and he and his friends were dancing. I walked through them back to Lucy and Estelle.

"So where did you two meet?" said Estelle.

We looked at each other and Lucy smiled. "Through friends," she said.

"Cool," said Estelle.

When it got hot and unbearably loud inside the store, Lucy and I went out and sat on the stoop.

"So," said Lucy. "College sweetheart?"

"No. Grad school sweetheart," I said, wanting to give her something.

"What did you go for?"

"Law," I said.

"Law? By grad school you mean law school?"

"Yup."

"What are you doing here, then?"

"I don't really know," I said.

"That's okay," she said.

We sat in silence for a minute and Lucy smiled at me.

"What about you?" I said. "College sweetheart?"

"Yeah," she said.

"What happened?" I said.

"You know," she said. She told me they moved to San Francisco for the girlfriend's job, they got a dog, they found a cat in the garbage. They were going to play "Here Comes the Bride" twice at their wedding, once for each of them. Then the girlfriend started spending a lot of nights at the office, and then it turned out she was coming home during the day to sleep with their downstairs neighbor.

"Shit," I said.

"Yeah," said Lucy.

While we were both thinking about her story, Pam came out of the store and put on her helmet. I put my head on Lucy's shoulder and smiled at Pam.

"You girls have fun." Pam got on her motorcycle and rode away. I picked my head up.

"She is kind of scary," said Lucy. She took a breath. "You probably want to make a run for it, hearing all this crap."

"It's really fine." I didn't want to make a run for it, but I did want to go home and see Danny.

"I'm still mad," she said. "Isn't that crazy? I'm mad at my

ex but I'm even madder at that girl. I didn't think I had it in me, but if I heard that she died I would honestly be glad."

I didn't say anything.

"You are so freaked out right now. You can honestly leave me here, I won't be offended."

"I'm not freaked out," I said. "It makes sense."

"It does? My friends think I am seriously unhinged."

"Then they haven't been cheated on."

She turned to me. "Have you?"

"No. But my dad cheated on my mom."

"Shit."

"It's fine. She's better off without him."

We sat quietly for a minute and then Marc came out and yelled, "Birthday cake!"

Everybody inside seemed significantly drunker.

"Okay," said Lucy, "we either need to do shots or get out of here."

"I should actually probably get home," I said.

"Oh yeah," she said, "me too."

We cut pieces of cake and watched Chad's boyfriend feed him, which was sweet, even though Chad was dripping with sweat and seemed to be on something other than alcohol. He was flexing his pecs to the beat of the music while he was taking bites.

Lucy called two cabs and we ate our cake slowly until we heard the cars honk. I waved to no one in particular and we left.

Outside Lucy said, "I really had fun."

I looked at her and smiled. "I did too." But suddenly it felt like we were standing too close to each other, so I looked away.

"Okay," she said.

Lucy opened the door to the first cab and motioned for me to get in. I took a step forward and she put her hand on my back. The warmth of her hand spread up to my scalp and down my legs. Maybe it shouldn't have felt like that, but no one had touched me in weeks.

At home I turned on the light in the bedroom, and Danny sat up and said, "I'm awake!"

"Babe," I said. "I didn't think you'd be here."

"Hm," he said and sunk back into the pillow.

I got into bed and pulled Danny's arm over me. He snuggled closer and kissed my neck.

On Saturday morning we woke up at the same time and Danny wrapped his arms around me. "Where were you last night?" he said.

"At Chad's birthday party at the store," I said. "I didn't know you were going to be home."

"I got home pretty late." Then he startled. "Oh my god!"

"What?" I said.

"Your hair."

"Oh yeah," I said, "my hair. Didn't you get my text?"

"No, I didn't get your text."

"I got a mullet. I got a mullet for you and you didn't even check your phone."

He touched the hair on the back of my head. Then he lifted up different sections and let them fall.

"How does it look?" I said.

"You look beautiful," he said.

I put my head in his armpit and my hand in his boxers. He laughed and tried to pull it out, but I held on for dear life and quickly got him to the point of no return. I climbed on top of him and he slowed down to wait for me.

Afterward I wanted him to do what he used to do on Sunday mornings, which was go down on me until he was ready to go again, but instead he said, "I'm starving. I can't remember eating anything yesterday."

We took separate showers and then walked to brunch and waited forever and finally ordered our eggs Benedict. Danny complained about some other first year whose wife had a baby months ago but who was still taking all this time off and not billing nearly enough hours. I guessed that was some kind of explanation, either for me or for himself. I told him about Chad's party, minus the part about Lucy.

"Do you honestly like working there?" he asked.

"Yes, I do," I said.

"Okay, well, I want to say one thing," he said. "Whatever you want to do, I will support you. But you don't have to do anything. You don't have to work. I know you think you have to but you don't."

"We need the money," I said.

"We don't need the money," he said. "And even if we did, that job wouldn't help."

"That's not very nice," I said. "What would I do if I quit?"

"Whatever you want," he said. "Volunteer for legal aid."

"That would make my dad happy," I said.

"Is that why you're doing this? To make your dad unhappy?"

"No."

"Then why are you doing it?"

"It's not my fault I can't get a law job."

"You're not applying for law jobs."

"I applied for two," I said.

"You don't even want a law job."

"Whatever," I said.

"Come on, babe, I want you to be happy. You could quit. We could get a dog."

"Well if we're going to get a dog, we might as well get a baby," I said, sort of joking but sort of not really.

"Ha," said Danny. "Let's start with a dog. A little rodent one like you want."

"Fine," I said.

. . .

On Monday I went to work with my head spinning. I wondered if I should quit, or if Pam was going to fire me first. I was giving myself a neck massage with the Hitachi Magic Wand when my dad walked through the open door and then walked right back out.

I followed him. He looked smaller and older than I remembered. At first he just sputtered. Finally he managed to spit out, "Brenda." Then more sputtering and then, "I thought this was another one of your goddamn jokes."

I didn't have any words.

"Turn that goddamn thing off," he said. I realized I was still holding the vibrating Magic Wand and that the cord was what had prevented me from getting farther outside. I switched it off and put it on the floor inside the door.

"I tried to tell you it wasn't a joke," I said.

"What in the hell are you thinking?"

"I need a job."

"You're a licensed attorney in the state of California."

"Yes, I remember," I said. "What are you doing here?"

"I came up to see a client," he said. "I went to your apartment."

"Good thing I gave you this address," I said.

"You and your goddamn jokes, Brenda. You think life is so goddamn funny."

"Actually I don't," I said. "I don't think it's funny at all."

A motorcycle stopped in front of the store, and for the first time I was glad to see Pam.

"How can you live like this?"

"I don't know."

Pam took her helmet off and approached us.

"You're throwing away your life."

"Why do you even care what I do?" I said. "Don't you just want me to be happy?"

"Not if this is what makes you happy," said my dad.

"I think you need to leave, sir," said Pam.

My dad looked at Pam. "Jesus Christ," he said.

"It's okay," I said. "This is my dad. He was just leaving."

He turned around and left without saying anything.

"Oh my god," said Pam. "Are you okay?"

"Yeah," I said.

"I am so sorry," she said.

It took me a second to understand why she was sorry.

"It's okay," I said.

"It's not okay," she said. "I feel awful. That was awful. No one should ever have to go through that."

"It's really okay," I said. "He's a dick."

"I'm very upset," she said.

"Don't be," I said. "I'm totally fine."

"He doesn't deserve to have you as a daughter."

"Yeah, that wasn't about me being gay," I said.

"What?" said Pam.

"That wasn't about me being gay."

"I think it was," she said.

"I'm not gay," I said.

Pam stared at me. Finally she shook her head and said, "Damn it."

"Sorry," I said.

She didn't say anything.

"Am I fired?" I said.

"I think so, yes," she said.

"I'm really good at pretending I'm gay," I said.

"You're really not. Not even with the haircut."

"So?"

"So lesbians don't want to buy sex toys from straight women."

"Oh," I said.

"I hope Eunice can come back," said Pam.

"Me too," I said.

"Why is that on the floor?" Pam pointed to the Magic Wand.

"I was massaging my neck," I said.

She started to walk back to the street.

"Did you stop by for a reason?" I said.

She turned around. "Just wanted to check on you, say thanks for coming to the party."

. . .

When Danny got home that night, he said my dad had called him to tell him that I was wasting my life and that he should do something about it.

"We might not see him again for a while," I said.

"That's fine," said Danny.

That Saturday, Danny took me to an animal shelter in Pacific Heights. He'd made his assistant look for dogs, and she had found one that she thought was perfect. I wanted to find my own dog, now that I was unemployed, but I agreed to go look.

When we got there, I told the woman I needed a dog to replace my fiancé.

"Ha, she's kidding," said Danny. "We're looking for a dog named Ruth?"

She brought us to a cage with a little nothing, ten or twelve pounds of stringy brown hair. I said hi, and the dog started throwing herself into the walls of the cage.

"Whoa," said Danny.

"She'll calm down," the woman said. Now Ruth was panting hysterically, and her tongue was hanging out one side of her mouth. The woman said it was because they'd had to remove her diseased teeth, which was all of them. She took her out of the cage and handed her to me.

The dog clung to my chest. Without any warning, I started to cry.

Danny put his hand on my back while I sobbed.

"We'll take this dog," he said to the woman.

When everything was settled we got a cab and I cried all the way home. The dog sat on my lap, shaking.

"It's okay," I told her. "It's okay."

PEARL AND
THE SWISS GUY
FALL IN LOVE

I hadn't had sex in over a year, partly because I didn't like anyone I met on the internet and partly because I adopted a pit bull who wouldn't let men into my apartment. In August I decided to try again and agreed to meet a Swiss guy at a bar that served Swiss absinthe. It was hot as fuck outside, and as soon as I got out of the subway, sweat started collecting on my lower back and between my boobs. I stopped to mop myself off and got a text from the Swiss guy that said, "I conquered us places at the bar!"

When I got there he stood up and waved. He was wearing round, very Swiss glasses. He had a goatee, but he had a great smile. He kissed me on both cheeks and we sat down. We started talking and couldn't stop. The bartender kept coming over to get our order, but we kept forgetting to look at the menu. Finally we ordered whatever fancy drinks we could pick out on the spot.

The Swiss guy had a PhD in economics, and he was in New York doing a postdoc on wage inequality and the American gender gap. He was thirty-six, which meant he was an actual adult. He showed me pictures of his two brothers and their families, and it seemed like he loved them all a lot. He wanted to know everything about me, which was a nice change of pace from the dates where I couldn't get a word in edgewise. He was especially excited that I was a teacher because his mom was a teacher. I thought that was sweet, even though she had taught kindergarten in rural Switzerland forty years earlier, and I taught humanities in an inner-city middle school with metal detectors and police.

We each had another drink. When I got up to go to the bathroom, I realized I was tipsy. I made my way to the back of the bar in a heightened state and then sat on the toilet, peeing and thinking I might marry this guy. If he didn't want to stay in the U.S., I didn't hate the idea of living as an ex-pat in Switzerland. I was enjoying the Swiss absinthe and I also liked cheese, chocolate, and mountains. When I washed my hands I noticed that the neckline of my dress was way too low. I fixed it and when I got back to the bar I apologized for my wardrobe malfunction.

"I like it very much," said the Swiss guy. "You have a beautiful décolletage."

"Should we get another drink?" I said.

We each ordered one more and then asked for the bill. He got out his credit card and I got out mine.

"Shall we split it?" he said. "That's very nice of you. I thought in America the guy had to pay."

"We can split it," I said.

We left and started kissing as soon as the door closed behind us.

"I don't usually make out in the street," I said.

"It's okay," he said.

"Can we at least go around the corner?" I said.

Around the corner there was a stoop.

"Sit down," I said.

"Is it dirty?" he said. "I think it's too dirty."

"Do you want to make out or not?"

He sat down and I straddled him and we kept going.

I knew it was past one in the morning and I should go home, but I was full of absinthe and it had been a long time since I had made out with anyone and it felt good. I told him that I had to go home to walk my dog, and we made out for a while longer.

"I could come to your house," he said.

"I don't think so."

"Why?"

"I just met you."

We got up and started walking.

"It would be nice to go home together," he said.

"I never have sex on the first date," I said.

"We don't have to have sex," he said. "We could just coddle."

"Cuddle?" I said. "No. Even if I wanted to, my dog has problems. I can't just show up with a stranger."

I had adopted Pearl a year earlier. She was a beautiful cream-colored pit, and she had been on death row at animal control because she was so scared that they couldn't do a behavior evaluation on her. But when I went to meet her she approached me with her tail wagging and she licked my face. I begged them to try the evaluation again, and the behavior supervisor conducted it herself. Soon I realized that that was the only reason Pearl passed—she was fine with women but very scared of and very aggressive toward men.

"Why can't you just show up with a stranger?" the Swiss guy said.

"You would scare her," I said. "And she would bite you."

He considered this. "Can she go in a different room? I'm a bit afraid of dogs."

"No," I said. "You can't come over."

"Okay," he said. "What is the dog's name?"

"Pearl."

"What kind of dog is she?"

"She's a pit bull."

"Bwah, then she will definitely bite me."

"She's not going to bite you because she's a pit bull. She's going to bite you because you're an intruder."

"Fine, so I don't come. What are you going to do tomorrow?"

"I don't know yet."

"I'm going to go upstate to do some research. You could come with me and we could stay in a motel."

"I can't leave Pearl."

"It would only be for one night."

"It doesn't work that way."

We got to the subway and started kissing again.

"Good-bye," I said.

"Good-bye," he said.

"Good-bye," I said and pushed him toward the subway. I hailed a cab. I should have taken the subway too, but I didn't like walking back from my stop late at night. When I got home, I took Pearl out and then we both ate some strawberry ice cream.

The next morning I had a text from the Swiss guy saying that it was raining so he wasn't going to go upstate, and did I want to hang out. I went to his apartment on the Upper West Side. The rain had cooled things off a little, but I still worked up a sweat climbing his six flights of stairs. He opened the door and gave me a kiss on my way in. I asked him for a glass of water and when I finished it he refilled it. The air in the apartment was hot and still. There was no couch to sit on but there was a wide chair without arms. We both sat on it, close together so we didn't fall off.

We didn't have quite as much to say as we had the night before. I felt the stiffness between us but I didn't know what it was—sexual tension, nonsexual tension, or the exertion of staying on the chair. Since we were side by side, the only way we could look at each other was by turning our necks, and when we did our faces were very close together.

I kept drinking water but I couldn't cool down. Finally I couldn't take the suspense anymore and suggested that we go into the Swiss guy's bedroom.

He kissed me and we lay down on the bed.

"Is this an air mattress?" I said.

"No, it's not," he said.

We started making out. I felt the sweat start seeping back through my skin. We took our clothes off.

"Would you like to sleep with me?" whispered the Swiss guy.

It took me a second to understand what he meant, and then I wanted to laugh because what the fuck else were we going to do.

"Sure," I said. "Do I have anything to worry about?"

"What do you mean?"

"Like have you been tested for STDs?"

"Yes."

"When?"

"Last year."

"Have you slept with anyone since then?"

"Just one woman."

"Do you have a condom?"

"Yes, I do. But have you been tested?"

"Yeah, I got tested last month and I haven't been with anyone in a long time."

"Okay."

I wouldn't exactly say it was magical, but for the first time with somebody I had known for less than twenty-four hours, it was pretty good. The Swiss guy had a great dick— thick and uncircumcised. I didn't think I would get tired of one like that.

Afterward we lay there, sweating and talking. Eventually he went to get more water, and I sat up and saw an air conditioner in the far window.

"Oh my god, you have an air conditioner?" I called.

He came back in. "Yes, I do."

"You're kidding me."

"Would you like me to turn it on?"

"I would love that."

He did and the air conditioner started buzzing, and soon I felt the first breaths of cool air on my feet.

We lay there.

"How is this for you?" he said.

"How is what?"

"How is it to have an affair?"

"What do you mean, 'affair'?"

"I mean because we are meeting now and I will be leaving."

"You mean a fling? You're going to be here for a while."

"I am leaving in one month."

"To go where?"

"Back to Switzerland."

"Forever?"

"Perhaps. I like to come back but I don't know if I will be allowed to."

I felt stung. "Why didn't you tell me yesterday?"

"I did."

He had said he was leaving when his program ended, but since the school year was about to start, I'd assumed he had at least one more year.

"When is your program over?"

"At the end of August, and then I am staying one more month after. I will go to California for two weeks and then I will return to New York for two weeks."

We lay quietly for a few minutes, and the sweat cooled on my skin.

On the subway home I tried not to cry. I wondered if it was time for my period, or if I was actually sad.

. . .

The next day was Saturday and when I woke up I had
another text from the Swiss guy. He was coming to Brooklyn for a party and wanted to meet up beforehand. I suggested going for a walk with my dog, because that's what
we had to do before she would let men into the apartment.
The Swiss guy said in that case I could come to his apartment. I asked if he only wanted to hang out if we could
have sex. He said of course not. I said good, because if he
was coming to Brooklyn anyway I was definitely not going
to go into the city.

The Swiss guy came to my neighborhood and Pearl and
I met him on a street where the sidewalks were wide and
where not a lot of people would walk by. I told him to stay
far away until I gave him instructions. He started to look
kind of pale.

"I'm quite afraid of dogs," he said.

"It's too late now," I said.

I threw him a bag of treats and told him to toss them
to Pearl from a distance. He looked at the treats through
the bag. He clearly didn't want to touch them. He hesi-
tantly threw one. Pearl gobbled it up and looked at him.
She was making progress. She wasn't barking or lunging.
She was getting better at identifying men who threw
treats as friends, but I was tired of having to do the intro-
ductions and was starting to dream about going to live

with her on some kind of feminist or lesbian all-women commune.

I told the Swiss guy to keep throwing treats. Pearl was getting closer and closer to him, wagging her tail, but he kept jumping back.

"You're doing fine," I said. "Give her some of the cheese."

"I don't like to touch it," he said.

"That's what will really make her like you," I said. "And you're already touching dehydrated lamb lung."

"What?"

"Just keep throwing the treats."

Now Pearl was sitting at his feet, thumping her tail, and the Swiss guy was trying to stay calm but not doing a good job. When I was sure that Pearl wasn't going to change her mind and eat him, we started walking. Pearl was excited about the Swiss guy until we got to the park, and then she switched her attention to the squirrels.

After the walk we dropped Pearl off at my apartment and got a quick dinner. I told the Swiss guy to speak to me in Swiss-German. I couldn't understand what he was saying, but his voice was sexier—deeper and more sure.

He left to go to his party, and a couple of hours later he texted me to ask if I wanted him to stop by again. I said sure, and when he got there Pearl and I went outside to meet him. Pearl recognized him immediately and started jumping and twisting in the air. The Swiss guy shrieked a little shriek.

"It's okay," I said. "She's just excited to see you."

We went inside and into the living room. I sat on the couch and the Swiss guy sat on the floor with Pearl. At first she tried to get in his face and lick him, but then she lay down next to him and let him rub her belly. We sat like that and talked for several hours, and he rubbed her the whole time. Then he got up and washed his hands and his arms and we went into the bedroom.

"Is Pearl going to be in the room?" he said.

"Is that okay?" I said. "She'll cry and cry if I shut her out. She won't bother us."

"Maybe she can stay on the floor."

I didn't think that was going to happen, and it didn't. But as soon as we lay down she went to the bottom of the bed and stayed very still until we were done.

When the Swiss guy sat up he said, "Is Pearl sleeping?"

"Yes."

"Is she angry with us?"

"No. How could she be angry? She's asleep."

She woke up when we got up. The Swiss guy asked if he could sleep on the couch. He was afraid that Pearl was going to kill him when he was asleep and defenseless. I got him a blanket and a pillow and escorted him out to the living room. Back in my bed, I spooned with Pearl.

In the morning the Swiss guy had to leave to meet a friend. I made him some coffee and told him to smell the milk in the fridge before he poured it. He didn't like the way it smelled, so he drank the coffee black. I also made him some muesli and yogurt, but he didn't want it even though he was Swiss.

It was the last time I was going to see him before he left for California. He had a few more days before he left, but he had to move out of his apartment and put his stuff in storage. He said he was going to try to find a cheap room when he got back to New York. He seemed stressed out.

"How much stuff do you have?" I said.

"About two large bags," he said.

"I know this sounds crazy, but you could stay here when you get back," I said. "You could leave your bags here."

"That's very kind of you, but I have only known you for four days."

"I know," I said. "Okay."

"But we will see each other when I return."

"Okay," I said.

He kissed me. I put my hand on his arm, but he pulled his arm away.

"What's wrong?"

"You touched Pearl and then you touched me."

"Uh," I said. "She's not really that dirty."

"I don't know," he said.

I washed my hands and he kissed me again.

"Okay," he said. "Good-bye. Good-bye, Pearl." He waved at her. She wagged her tail.

. . .

I waited to hear from the Swiss guy. I wondered if I even was going to hear from him, and if it was possible to fall in love in four days and two weeks. I wondered if wanting to talk to him plus wanting to listen to him plus being satisfied with his man parts equaled love.

I couldn't text the Swiss guy myself, because that was against the rules as laid out by my younger brother. A couple of years earlier he had explained that a girl should never initiate contact with a guy. If a guy contacts you first you can write back, but you should never make the first move. My brother said it was basic human psychology— the less you contact a guy, the more he wonders about you, and the more he wonders about you, the more he thinks he likes you. I had been following my brother's instructions and they seemed to be working fine. I liked avoiding guys not writing me back by not writing them in the first place.

School started and the Swiss guy finally wrote to say he had met another nice dog on his travels. He sent me a picture of it. He asked if I wanted to hang out that week when he was back. Then he said he was getting in the next morning and didn't have anywhere to go. I did the math and figured that he was already at the airport in California. I said I agreed that he shouldn't stay with me, but if he wanted he could come over in the morning and stay for a night or two while he looked for a room. He said we could talk about it when he got there, and I felt embarrassed for offering again.

I went to bed late, and I could hardly sleep with the promise of sex running through my body. Finally the Swiss guy called to say he was downstairs, and Pearl and I went down to meet him. Pearl recognized him through the front door and went bananas.

Back upstairs the Swiss guy and I had sex, he went to sleep on the couch, we woke up and had sex again, he left to go do research at the library, and when he came back we had sex again.

On Monday he was scared to be home alone with Pearl so he went to a coffee shop when I went to school. That evening I met up with him and we went to a Mexican restaurant in my neighborhood. The Swiss guy balked at the health department rating of B, but I told him that all the restaurants in the neighborhood had Bs, and that the only difference between a B restaurant and an A restaurant was that the A restaurant got lucky during their inspection. He told me all about his trip to California and then he started talking about how he was leaving forever. I said I really wished he had told me before we met, or at least when we met. He said he was sorry and told me about a successful fling he had when he was traveling in Asia. The girl was German and he said they traveled around together and had a nice time. Now she was married and had a baby.

"So you do this a lot?" I said.

"No, not a lot," he said. "That was the first time and this is the second time."

"Great."

I waited for him to explain how this was different from the first time, but he moved on to telling me what research he still needed to do before he left. He was eating and drinking very slowly, and eventually we were the last people in the restaurant.

When we got home I told him I needed a minute and went into my bedroom and cried. Pearl lay with me. When I thought I could control myself I went into the bathroom and washed my face. The Swiss guy was sitting in the living room, waiting for me to help him use my illegal portable washing machine, and now Pearl was sitting next to him on the couch.

"Have you been sleeping?" he said.

"No. Where's the laundry you want to do?"

"Are you feeling sad?" he said.

"No," I said, and went back to the bathroom to cry a little more.

When I came out he wanted to talk about it.

"There's nothing to talk about," I said. "I think I'm going crazy right now."

"You're not crazy," he said.

I got into bed and he followed me. Pearl curled up between us.

"Why are you feeling sad?" he said.

"Because I'm crazy and because I never meet anyone I don't hate. And I don't hate you but you're leaving."

"It's sad for me too," he said. "I don't want to leave. But it's very difficult to stay in America without a job."

"I know. It's okay. We don't have to talk about it."

"We can if you like to."

"I don't want to."

We did his laundry and then got back in bed and had sex. After, I asked him if he wanted to sleep in the bed and solemnly swore that Pearl wouldn't kill him, but he said he wasn't ready.

I felt better the next day. We agreed to meet outside the library after school and get groceries and make dinner at home. He hadn't said anything about finding a room.

When I got to the library there was a crowd standing over someone on the ground. I called the Swiss guy to find him. He was standing up the block. He said the guy was on the ground because a lot of kids kicked him and then ran away. He said he didn't do anything because at first he thought the kids were playing and then when he realized they weren't, he didn't want them to attack him too.

While we were standing there a fire truck and an ambulance pulled up to the curb.

"Here's the fire truck," I said.

"Why is there a fire truck?"

"For that guy."

"But why does he need a fire truck?"

"He doesn't, but they always send one."

"Should I go and tell them what I have seen?"

"I doubt it would help."

"It was a big group of teenagers and they went that way." He pointed up the street.

"It's too late now," I said. "I'm sure they're long gone." I couldn't believe the Swiss guy watched the whole thing and did nothing. Even if he was too scared to intervene, he could have at least called the police.

We started walking.

"Is it very dangerous in this neighborhood?" he said.

"No. I've never seen anything like that happen before. And those kids probably knew each other."

We stopped to get groceries and I paid for them. When we got home Pearl was very excited to see us, especially the Swiss guy. She danced around him. He asked me what I thought she did while we were gone. I said I didn't know. I took her out and then I made a stir-fry with the vegetables we bought and a pepper I already had.

"Is that pepper still good?" said the Swiss guy.

"Yeah," I said. "I bought it a few days ago."

He talked and talked about applying for fellowships and jobs. He said it was hard for people to get a job in their field in Switzerland, especially if their field was academic. We ate in the kitchen and I sat on a high stool and he sat on a chair. Looking down at him I noticed that his hair was thinning and the scalp underneath was shiny.

After dinner we had sex. I now understood that he had two signature moves, neither of which I particularly liked. One was patting my vagina, which he must have learned from a porno. The other was swiveling his hips in what felt like a circle. To get him to stop the patting I initiated sex, and to get him to stop the circles I offered to get on top.

Afterward he wanted to talk about Pearl. She was curled up at the bottom of the bed and her eyelids were twitching.

"Is she dreaming?" he said.

"I guess so."

"What is she dreaming about?"

"I don't know."

"Maybe she is dreaming about squirrels."

"Maybe."

When he was done watching Pearl, he went to go sleep on the couch.

On Friday night the Swiss guy met a friend for dinner and I was glad for the silence. I was starting to wonder when he was going to leave, but I still wanted to have sex. Before he got home I put on a lacy chemise.

"That's a nice pajama," he said when he got there. "Shall I come visit you in your room for a while?"

We lay down and started making out. Then he licked the roof of my mouth. I jerked my head back but he tried to put his tongue back in to do it again. I started to touch him but he started patting my vagina.

"That doesn't feel good."

He kept doing it. He was supporting my theory that most guys touch vaginas to turn themselves on, and are not really concerned with what feels good to the vagina. I thought the Swiss guy would be different. I moved his hand.

"That doesn't feel good," I said.

"Okay," he said. "What can I do then?"

"Mouths feel good," I said.

"What?" he said.

"You could use your mouth."

"What?"

"Oral sex?" I said. "Not happening?"

"Well we haven't been tested."

"I've been tested."

"But you haven't been tested for everything."

"There's no way to test for everything."

"I would like to wait until we can be tested for everything. I am worried about getting throat cancer like Michael Douglas."

Another time I would have laughed, but I was not in the mood.

"Okay," I said. "Never mind."

I put lube on myself and then tried to put it on him, but he jumped away.

"Do you mind going to wash your hands?" he said.

"I haven't touched Pearl at all," I said.

"But you touched yourself and now you want to touch me."

"Okay." I got up and washed my hands. I was all for safe sex, and I definitely wasn't going to blow the Swiss guy when he hadn't been tested, but I had been tested and him freaking out anyway was starting to make me feel like my vagina was crawling with carcinogens.

When I got back with my hands clean we started having sex. Then he asked me if I wanted to do it from behind, and I said okay because I always want to do it from behind. I know it's supposed to be degrading but it's a good angle. But this time the Swiss guy started doing something different. It was like he was both behind me and on top of me, and something was putting pressure on my back.

"You're hurting my back," I said.

"What is hurting?" he said, out of breath.

"You're hurting my back," I said.

"Okay," he said, and stopped whatever he was doing.

A little while later he started trying to do it again.

"You're going to break my back," I said. I moved forward to get out from under him. I turned over and let him in again from the front.

"I'm not going to come," I said. "You can go ahead."

"Are you certain?" he said.

"Yes, I'm certain."

He did his circle thing until he came.

He went to the bathroom and when he came back he said, "I think I can sleep in the bed with you and Pearl tonight."

He sat on the edge of the bed and put his pajamas on, long pants and a turtleneck. He got under the covers and we slept on opposite sides of Pearl, him in his pajamas and me naked.

The next morning he woke me up.

"It's Saturday," I said. "Please don't wake me up."

He left me alone for a little while and then came back and started talking to me again.

"Do you need something?" I said.

"No," he said.

"Okay," I said. "Then please don't wake me up." But it was too late; I was awake. I kept my eyes closed until I heard him leave the apartment, and then I got up.

That night I told him I had a lot of work to do and shut myself and Pearl in my room. Pearl cried on my side of the door. I told her the Swiss guy wasn't all he was cracked up to be. I told her he was prejudiced against pit bulls. When it was time for bed the Swiss guy said that he hadn't been sleeping well on the couch, and could he sleep in the bed again. I didn't want it to seem like I was punishing him for licking the roof of my mouth, so I said fine. But the next night I locked the door to my bedroom before he got home.

The less I talked to him, the more the Swiss guy talked to me. He mostly wanted to talk about Pearl. If she was awake he wanted to know if she was sleepy. If she was sleeping he wanted to know if she was really sleeping or if it just looked like she was. He wanted to know if she was hungry, and I pointed out that she had a huge bowl of food on the floor, and if she wanted to she could eat the whole damn thing. Instead she liked to eat a couple of kibbles every hour or so. The Swiss guy wanted to know why. One day he asked me if Pearl was going to work with me. I said no, she definitely couldn't go to school, and he wanted to know why not.

In addition to talking about himself and talking about Pearl, he liked to talk about my kitchen. He didn't like that I let the dishes pile up, and tried to convince me that it was better to wash them right away. He was also very concerned with whether my food was still good. I made macaroni and cheese and he wanted to know if the cheese he grated for me was still good, even though it had come straight from the wrapper. He wanted to know if the eggs I used were still good, and if the oil I made the potatoes in was still good. He did buy groceries once: more milk for his coffee, a tin of cookies, and a bottle of wine product. The wine product was made of California table wine, water, sugar, concentrated juice, natural fruit flavors, citric acid, and carbon dioxide.

I pretty much stopped talking to the Swiss guy, but Pearl didn't. They spent a lot of time sitting on the couch together. He let her sit on his lap and he talked to her in a baby voice, asking her questions about herself. Once I caught him letting her lick his ear. He was laughing, and all of a sudden she licked his open mouth. I could only hope that Pearl had HPV all over her tongue.

I started going to bed at seven or eight, before the Swiss guy came home, and leaving before he got up in the morning. I didn't see him at all for several days. I told my brother that I was running a homeless shelter out of my apartment, and he offered to come down to the city to invite the Swiss guy to leave. My brother was an amateur MMA fighter and worked as a bouncer, and he was good at inviting people to do things he wanted them to do. I should have taken him up on it, because I didn't have the guts to do it myself. It was only a few more days until the Swiss guy was flying back, and letting him stay seemed better than having to talk to him to ask him to leave. He did end up offering to leave, several days after I stopped speaking to him and two days before he was going to leave anyway. I told him not to bother.

Then the Swiss guy mentioned that there was a chance he would be able to make a last-minute presentation at a conference in New York in two weeks. He wondered if he should change his ticket. I wondered what would happen if he tried to stay. I googled "how to evict a guest." I didn't mean evict literally, but it turned out that in some cases you did actually have to evict guests. If they stayed for thirty days, they would establish residency and you would have to legally evict them. And even before thirty days, if you asked someone to leave and they didn't, and you changed the locks and put their bags outside, they could say that you had a verbal agreement and sue you for unlawful eviction.

I called my brother back and told him that I really didn't need him to come down, but I was just wondering what he would do if I did.

He said he would ask the Swiss guy to leave.

"But what if he didn't leave?"

"I wouldn't give him the choice."

"What do you mean?"

"I would tell him that it was time for him to leave, and if he didn't leave on his own I would help him."

"What do you mean you would help him?"

"I would give him whatever incentive he needed to leave, and if he still didn't leave I would make it very uncomfortable for him to stay. And if he gave me a reason to remove him physically, I would do that."

"Okay."

"Do you need me to come down?"

"No, not yet."

. . .

The Swiss guy wanted to take me out to eat to thank me for my hospitality. By that point I felt that the only way he could thank me was to fall off the face of the earth. He countered any excuse I gave with a different time or a different place. Finally, to get him to stop asking, I said maybe to breakfast on Saturday, the day before he was supposed to leave. He hadn't said anything else about changing his ticket, but he hadn't said anything about keeping it either. On Friday night when he wanted to confirm our breakfast plans, I told him that it was still maybe. I told him I didn't know what time I would be up, and that he shouldn't wake me unless the apartment was on fire.

On Saturday morning I woke up having to pee and looked at my watch. It was only eight twenty, and I was half proud of myself for getting up so early, and half crushed that I would have to face the Swiss guy so early. I lay in bed trying to control my bladder, and wondering if I could get to the bathroom and back without him knowing I was awake. Finally I couldn't wait any longer. I left Pearl in the bedroom. I peed and then peeked into the living room. The Swiss guy wasn't there.

I went back to my bedroom and wondered where he had gone so early in the morning. I looked at my phone to see if he had texted me. He had. Then I noticed that my phone said it was two fifty in the afternoon. I looked back at my watch and realized I had looked at it upside down, and it was in fact two fifty.

The Swiss guy's texts said that he was leaving for the library, and then that he was at the library, and then he was wondering if I was going to meet him or not, because he was so hungry. I texted him back saying I guessed it wasn't a good day. He said he'd been waiting for me. I felt kind of bad and decided it was worth the free pancakes if I only had to show up, eat them, and leave. To expedite things I told him to go ahead and order, but the food arrived quicker than I calculated, and by the time I got there he was done eating and my pancakes were cold. I ate them as fast as I could and he talked about how he really wanted to stay in New York for the conference, but if he didn't go back to Switzerland he would lose those two weeks of unemployment pay. I couldn't bear the sound of his voice.

Afterward I went to walk around Target for a few hours. When I got home the Swiss guy wasn't there. I went to bed excited and anxious about the next day. The Swiss guy's flight back to Switzerland was at eight p.m.

In the morning I stayed in my room until the Swiss guy left to get his stuff from his storage unit. He texted to say he would be back around two and had to leave for the airport at five, so I took Pearl out for a walk at one forty-five and got back at five fifteen. We had never walked so many miles in our lives. At five fifteen the Swiss guy was still there, packing. I offered to help him but he said he was almost done, so I offered to call him a cab. I saw the keys he had been using lying on the back of the couch and pocketed them. He knelt down to say good-bye to Pearl and they kissed each other. I helped the Swiss guy carry his stuff down the stairs.

When the cab came, we said good-bye.

"Thank you very much for everything." He gave me a hug.

"No problem," I said.

"Let's keep in touch," he said.

"Okay," I said.

He waved from the cab as it pulled away, and I smiled. It had probably been at least a week since he had seen me smile.

Upstairs he had left a bunch of empties, and a set of glasses from Ikea and some towels that he wanted me to give to a good home. I told him I didn't want them, and he said, "As long as they go to someone who can use them, that's the important thing." I brought everything down to the garbage, and back upstairs I opened the wine product for the fruit flies that had been flying around the empties.

A few days later I forgot my phone at home and when I got back from school I had a million text messages from my brother.

"Hey."

"What's up?"

"How is everything?"

"Is everything okay?"

"Why are you ignoring me?"

"Write back so I know everything is okay."

"I'm getting worried."

"Write back or I'm calling Mom."

"Write back or I'm calling the police."

I called him. "I'm fine! Why are you freaking out?"

"Last I knew you had a strange man living in your apartment," he said. "How was I supposed to know he didn't kill you?"

"Swiss people don't kill people," I said. "If anybody had killed anybody, I would have killed him."

"So he's gone now?"

"Yeah, he's gone. He left on Sunday. The happiest day of my life."

"Why did you let him stay if you didn't even like him?"

"I did like him," I said. "Until I got to know him better." I took off my pants and got into bed. Pearl jumped up and settled down with her body along my body, and her head on my shoulder.

"Please never do this again," said my brother.

"I won't," I said. "I will never date again."

When Pearl heard me say "bye" she thumped her tail. I snuggled into her, and she turned her head and brushed the side of my face with the tip of her tongue.

NEW GIRLS

Ernesta

When we moved to Germany, the real estate agent said there were tons of girls in the neighborhood for me to be friends with. She also said that I could take the bus to school from the bottom of the street, but it turned out that that bus stop had been out of service for years and the nearest stop was a kilometer away, which was really far at six o'clock in the morning when I was still asleep, and again after school when I was starving.

Obviously the real estate agent also lied about the girls. There were only two girls in the neighborhood, and they were hard to find. One supposedly lived across the street but I didn't see her for all of August. Her brothers claimed she was away. In the second week of August I found the other girl. I was outside watching my mom smoke a secret cigarette and pour beer on the slugs in the garden. A girl walked up to the gate and at first I thought she was older than me, and then I thought she was younger but a giant. She was very friendly and she spoke some English. Her name was Ernesta.

She invited me to go over to her house, which was four houses down from ours. I went back to my mom.

"I don't even know her," I said.

"It's okay," said my mom.

"You don't even know her parents," I said. "I can't go over to someone's house unless you know their parents."

"It will be okay," said my mom. "You'll be a few houses away. I'll be able to hear you if you scream."

"Mom! It's not safe."

"Everything in Germany is safe."

"How do you know?"

"Come on, Steph. Just go."

I went out to the sidewalk and Ernesta smiled. I followed her down the street. When we got to her house her mom was in the living room, ironing underwear. She smiled at me and said some German things, and Ernesta translated that she was glad to meet me. We went to Ernesta's room and played a game called Manhattan, where we tried to build the highest skyscraper with little parts of buildings.

In the next weeks we played Manhattan many times. While we were playing we had conversations using all the English words Ernesta knew and all the German words I knew. One day Ernesta asked me about the real Manhattan and if it was true that the models lived there. Ernesta said she might become a model because she was tall, but I wouldn't because I was so short. I tried to tell her I was going to grow more, but either she didn't understand or she didn't believe me. I thought I had a better chance of being a model than she did. She wasn't really pretty and also her name was Ernesta.

Lisa

At the end of August the missing girl came back. She had been on a teen tour to the UK. Her name was Lisa and she was tall and skinny and very tan. She spoke better English and had a better house than Ernesta. She had a huge room filled with magazines, and I spent the last weeks of the summer vacation looking at them. The only kids' magazines I read back in the States were *Ranger Rick* and some Christian magazines that my grandpa's wife subscribed me to. These German magazines were way better. They were for teenagers and they had "Fotoromane," which were like comics but with pictures of real people, and the people were sometimes kissing and sometimes even naked. I could hardly read any of the words but it didn't matter.

One day Lisa and I found an ad for a contest in one of the magazines. If you sent in a picture of your legs, you could win one thousand deutsche marks and a chance to be a model for a shaving cream company. We decided that Lisa should enter because her legs were tanner and more grown-up looking. She put on some very short shorts and I took pictures of her legs with a disposable camera. I didn't think her legs looked shiny enough, so she put lotion on them. They still didn't look shiny enough, so I suggested she put butter on them. Then her legs were super shiny. When we were done taking the pictures she tried to wash the butter off in the bathtub, but her legs were too slippery. She told me to go get her mom. Her mom didn't speak English, so Lisa told me what to say in German: *"Frau Schneider, Lisa hat Butter auf ihren Beinen."*

Brigitta

Finally it was time to go to school. Because my parents didn't love me or my brother, they were sending us to

German public school for the two years we were going to be in Germany. My brother could go to the elementary school in our town, but I had to take the bus from the faraway bus stop to a faraway city, thirty minutes away. My school was actually near the Mercedes-Benz offices where my dad was working, but he couldn't drive me because we had to go at different times. A couple of days before school started my parents said they were going to find me a friend to go to school with on the first day. It couldn't be Ernesta because she wasn't going to go to the same school as me, and I hadn't seen her much since Lisa got back anyway. It couldn't be Lisa because she was going into ninth grade and I was going into sixth. It had to be a girl in my class who could show me around.

My dad called the school and they gave him two names, one girl in our town and one in the next town over. He spent a long time consulting the dictionary and writing out what he wanted to say, and then he called the first girl's house. No one answered, so he left a message. The next day he called again, and on the third day he decided that they must be on vacation and he called the second girl. Her mom answered and said that her daughter would be happy to meet me and show me around. She said we could come over to their house the next day.

The next day we got lost on the way because my dad had written the directions in German, to practice. When we finally got there a pretty girl who spoke perfect English opened the door, and I felt like things were going to be okay. But she turned out to be Brigitta's older sister, and Brigitta herself did not speak, in English or in German. Brigitta was my same height and she had thick brown hair that hung over her face. Her mom came out and introduced us, but Brigitta just smiled a big smile full of braces. I was a little bit worried about having a mute guide, but I figured that it didn't really matter since we didn't speak the same language anyway. Brigitta's mom had made us a fruit tart, and she invited my dad to stay and eat. We sat at a table outside and Brigitta's sister asked me a million questions in English about America, and then she told me all about our school. She said the school was six hundred years old but I wouldn't notice because the buildings were very modern. She said she had the same teacher as us when she was in the sixth grade, and he was really nice. Brigitta sat and smiled. When we were done eating, the grown-ups went inside and we stayed out on the swings, and Brigitta's sister talked and Brigitta still just smiled.

On the first day of school I went in with Brigitta, and everyone crowded around us and asked me questions in English. They wanted to know where I was from and why I moved to Germany, and they wanted to know which language I was going to take and which religion class I was going to be in. For religion there were only two choices, *katholisch* and *evangelisch*. I wondered why there were no other choices. Almost all the kids in my old school were Jewish, except for one kid who was Zoroastrian. I didn't know what that meant and we didn't study either of those things. I tried to tell the kids I wasn't religious at all but they said I had to pick one. I picked *evangelisch* because I was sure I wasn't *katholisch*. Half of the class cheered, and I didn't know whether it was the *katholisch* half or the *evangelisch* half.

For language there were also two choices, *Englisch* and *Latein*. My mom and dad had a fight about which one I would take. My dad wanted me to take Latin, but my mom said it would be sadistic to make me take Latin when I didn't even speak German. I told the class I was going to take English, and again half the class cheered.

I ended up loving English because it was the only class where I understood anything. The English teacher didn't love me back, though, because she didn't like it when I helped her. Like when she told the class there was no English word for *Geschwister*, I raised my hand to say actually there was, and it was "siblings." I had learned the word *Geschwister* because that was one of the getting-to-know-you questions. What's your name, how old are you, where do you live, do you have any *Geschwister*?

Krystal

It turned out there was a boy in my class who spent summers in the States and spoke English fluently, and who happened to look just like Jonathan Taylor Thomas, my favorite actor. His name was Benjamin. I started hanging around him as much as I could so that I didn't have to speak German, and soon he was my boyfriend.

I hadn't had a boyfriend in a long time. In kindergarten I had a boyfriend named Joseph, who I was going to marry and have ten children with. But after kindergarten I went to a different school and everything went downhill. The boys ignored me and the girls made fun of me. It was a small private school and it was hard to stay out of the other kids' way. In first grade, the second-grade girls kicked me off the swings on the playground, meaning they kicked me until I got off the swings. In second grade one of the girls caught me singing songs from *The Little Mermaid* by myself, and they all made fun of me for that for the rest of the year. In third grade those girls said I could play hairdresser with them, and they cut off my ponytail with scissors. Fourth grade wasn't so bad because I stayed away from them at recess, and I was safe in my classroom because I was in a special class of kids who had it as bad as I did. I thought fifth grade would be even better because the mean girls were going to middle school, but I somehow made enemies with a new girl in my class, Krystal, who told me that I didn't wash my hair or clean the dirt out from under my nails. I didn't know what she was talking about because I did wash my hair and my nails were too short to have dirt under them. I spent all of fifth grade begging my mom to send me to public school, so that I could at least start over. My mom said no again and again, and then when she knew about moving to Germany she started saying, "Let's see what happens. You never know what might happen." So now I got to go to public school, except in another country and in a language I didn't speak.

Veronika and Viktoria

I was very happy about Benjamin being my boyfriend, until I started to understand that one of the two most popular girls in the class had had a crush on him for her whole life, and that was why the girls in the class weren't inviting me to go out to lunch with them. I thought it was just because I was unlikable, but they were actually mad at me.

The two most popular girls were twins named Veronika and Viktoria. They were half a year older and half a head taller than the rest of the class. They were kind of chubby but that didn't seem to matter. Everyone thought they were really cool because they smoked cigarettes and drank beer.

The twins had a sidekick named Ilona, and the three of them were the three most popular bad girls. Then there were three popular good girls, who were really smart and were in charge of stuff in the classroom. One was the other girl my dad tried to call, the one who lived in my town. I wondered if things would have been different if my dad had been able to reach her and she had been my first friend. Another one of those girls was some kind of tennis champion, and the third one was very small and the best in the class at every single subject.

Then there were three not popular but not unpopular girls. Nothing was wrong with them but they didn't seem to be special in any way. Then there was Brigitta, who the twins were protective of, because she lived in their neighborhood and had gone to their elementary school. And there was Monika Biermann, who loosened her retainer with her tongue and spit it onto her desk every time she was about to say something in class.

I wasn't exactly sure where I fit in, but I was pretty sure it wasn't good. I was okay with that when I thought girls in Germany just didn't like me, same as girls in America. But when it turned out that I had done something wrong and was being punished, I felt like I had ruined a perfectly good chance to be popular.

On the day we had afternoon classes, everyone went to one of four places. Almost no one went to the IBM cafeteria across the street. The food was actually pretty good but the cafeteria was full of adults. Then there was the Ikea down the street, and a McDonald's a couple of bus stops away, on my bus line. But most of the kids went to a mall called Breuningerland. I didn't know where it was or how they got there, so I couldn't tell my parents about it to get permission to go. Usually I went to the IBM cafeteria and read, and sometimes if Benjamin wasn't going to lunch with the boys or Brigitta wasn't going with the girls, one of them would go to the Ikea or the McDonald's with me. Benjamin especially liked to go to the Ikea to push each other around in the carts, which wasn't really what I imagined when I thought about going out to lunch with my boyfriend.

I was grateful to Brigitta for being the only girl who was nice to me, but I was starting to get tired of trying to talk to her. She technically could speak, but she didn't like to do it, and when she did it was hard for me to understand her because she was so quiet and because I still didn't really understand German.

I started saving the seat on the bus for Benjamin instead, who got on at the stop after Brigitta. On the weekends I mostly looked at magazines at Lisa's house, and sometimes Benjamin and I went on dates to the movies. Those dates weren't really what I hoped for either. I wasn't allowed to take the bus on the weekends so my mom would drive us, and Benjamin would ride in the backseat with my brother. One time we went to see *Romeo + Julia* but it was almost sold out and we couldn't get seats next to each other. Benjamin wanted to see *Independence Day* instead, but I thought *Romeo + Julia* would be more romantic. So we got seats near each other but in different rows, and I sat in front of Benjamin. I thought that would be close enough to hold hands but it wasn't.

Benjamin and I kept breaking up and getting back together, because he didn't want to French-kiss me because he thought it was gross, and because I purposely flirted with other boys on the bus. I sort of tried to stop doing it, but not really. No boys had ever talked to me before, and now they did, older boys from the eighth grade. I liked that and I kind of enjoyed how mad it made Benjamin. There were also smaller problems, like that for Christmas I got him a stuffed dog and he got me a nose horn. He got one for himself too. You put the nose horn up to your nose and snorted, and it played a note. I never played it but my mom did. She thought it was hilarious and she played it all the time, even though it made me mad.

In January the twin who loved Benjamin (Viktoria) passed out in class, and the other one (Veronika) was stumbling around, and it turned out they were taking diet pills and not eating. When the teacher talked to them about it they said it was because of me, because they wanted to be skinny like me. If they had asked me I would have told them that I would have preferred not to be so skinny and not to have to wear elastic-waist jeans. But they didn't ask.

Our teacher talked to me about the problem, but I still didn't understand German well, and I didn't understand why I needed to know that they were taking diet pills because of me, or what he wanted me to do about it. A lot was getting lost in translation, in and out of class.

In the spring I broke up with Benjamin for good, and then tried to get him back a few days later when I remembered that no one else in my class talked to me. He didn't want to get back together, so I made him a mixtape of the most romantic Backstreet Boys songs and rode my bike all the way to the next town and left it on his doorstep. When I called to see if he got it, his mom got on the phone and asked me in English to please leave her son alone.

After we broke up, all the girls wanted to talk to me to find out what happened and who I had a crush on now. They didn't exactly decide we were friends, but they seemed to be softening. If I had realized the solution to my problem was as simple as breaking up with Benjamin, I would have done it earlier.

In June my parents got me Backstreet Boys concert tickets for my birthday, and I asked the twin who liked Benjamin (Viktoria) if she wanted to go. She was the biggest Backstreet Boys fan in the class, and I hoped that the ticket would be irresistible and would make her forgive me. She said yes, and on the morning of the concert my mom and I got up at five in the morning, picked up Viktoria, and went to wait in line to get in. We were finally let into the arena in the afternoon, and we made it into the section closest to the stage, which was what we were hoping for. We packed into the crowd at the front, with my mom right behind us. When the opening act started, the crowd pushed forward, and Viktoria started to panic and had to be lifted out by security and taken to the medic's tent. My mom and I made our way out of the crowd to follow her, and when she was feeling better we went back to watch the rest of the concert from outside the crowd. On the way home she said thank you for inviting her, and from then on I was allowed to go to Breuningerland with the other girls in the class.

Ilona

By September I was starting to gain weight. I wasn't trying to, because I had already reached my goal of being able to wear regular jeans, but I had gotten into the habit of buying snacks after school, before I got on the bus or after I got off, or sometimes both. Back home I had never even been in a grocery store by myself, but now I could stop anywhere and get anything I wanted, and my favorite thing was these soft pretzels with butter. Maybe because of all the pretzels I started to get boobs, but to cancel them out I got braces.

My dad was also getting fat because he also liked those pretzels very much. My brother was the same as always, and my mom was getting skinny. She didn't really have anything to do while we were at school so she joined a gym and she went every day. Now she was even riding her bike to the gym because she couldn't drive anymore. She got to use her American license for the first year but then she had to take the German driving test, and she failed because the right-of-way rules in Germany made absolutely no sense. Luckily my dad passed his test or we would have all had to ride our bikes or the bus. Anyway, now my mom was really thin and had a lot of muscles.

On the first day of school it turned out that the twins' sidekick Ilona had somehow been dethroned. I didn't know what had happened, but I didn't care because Ilona asked me if I wanted to share a desk with her, and I obviously did. Ilona had really long black hair and she did her makeup like the older girls—she wore black lip liner on the outside of her lips and pale lipstick on the inside.

Natascha

Also on the first day of school, there was a new girl. Her name was Natascha, and Ilona and I saw right away that she was weird. Her clothes were different from everyone else's—they looked healthy. They weren't made of burlap but they were pretty close. Everything looked like it was made out of some kind of natural material and came from some kind of store that none of the rest of us had ever even been to. She had a high voice and spoke very quietly, and she moved in a funny way—her head bobbed when she talked. She was very thin and pale, and she wore thick glasses and had braces. She and her two older siblings rode their bikes to school every day, and she carried her helmet around with her. The food she ate was mostly really bad-smelling vegetables, like cabbage and brussels sprouts, and things my mom would say tasted like cardboard, like rice cakes and seed crackers.

At first no one knew what to do with her, so we didn't give her any trouble. But soon she started following groups of us to lunch. We didn't like it that she followed us without asking, and one day we decided to lose her on the way there. Ilona said she didn't want her to come, and I made a plan. I told everyone to run in a different direction as soon as the bell rang, and when we lost her we would meet back up at Ikea. If she did follow someone, they had to have lunch with her, alone, and they couldn't tell her where we were.

When the bell rang we took off, and I ran out the wrong door, around the building, and then to Ikea. When we all got there we were out of breath and laughing, and

Natascha was nowhere to be seen. We ate our lunch and then went back to school, and I didn't look at Natascha for the rest of the day.

At the end of the fall we took a class trip to the North Sea. It was a privilege that we earned for being in the seventh grade, and we had a fund-raising bake sale and our parents wrote checks and the teachers booked train tickets and a hostel. Our homeroom teacher and our religion teacher were going to come with us, since we needed a man and a woman. The religion teacher (*evangelisch*, not *katholisch*) was young, and she had the longest armpit hair I had ever seen. Ilona and I made jokes about it blowing in the wind, because it did.

We spent several weeks getting ready for the trip: going over the trains and making sleeping arrangements for the hostel. The girls' dorms had eight beds each, and there were thirteen girls in the class. It didn't end up being even because the twins picked six girls for their room, and the other five of us were in the other room—me, Ilona, Brigitta, Monika Biermann, and Natascha. Ilona had never recovered her rightful place with the twins, and instead she and I had become inseparable. We weren't happy about being stuck in the second room, especially because of Natascha and how weird she smelled. We made jokes

about how she was going to bring a whole suitcase just for
her giant maxi pads.

On the train ride to the North Sea, I hung out with
Benjamin. I wondered if maybe we were going to get back
together. He sat with his arm around me and I sort of
hoped we were because it felt nice to be close to someone.
Then he said he needed to ask me a question and whispered, "Will you have sex with me?" I told him no, and I
wondered what he would have done if I said yes, if he even
had any idea what to do. Even though I knew all about sex
from the magazines, it hadn't occurred to me to have sex
myself. But now I thought about how I wouldn't be able to
get pregnant because I hadn't gotten my period yet. My
answer was still no, but that was something that would
have been interesting about having sex then.

When we got to the hostel, it turned out that Natascha
did have a whole suitcase just for her maxi pads. It was a
small suitcase but the package was the only thing in it—a
maybe twelve-by-eighteen-inch package of the biggest,
healthiest pads on the planet. Ilona and I died laughing.
We couldn't believe that we had been right. Natascha's
other suitcase was half clothes and half healthy food that
her parents had packed her for the trip.

The five of us, but mostly me and Ilona, made a point
to sound like we were having a lot of fun in our room.
We laughed loudly all the time. One night we had a fake
orgasm contest until the religion teacher came to shut it

down. Natascha was trying to sleep with a pillow over her head and the other girls were giggling.

We spent the trip studying worms that lived in the sand, and on the last night we had a dance party in the basement of the hostel. Ilona danced with the boy she liked, and I watched her and everyone else for a while. Benjamin wasn't talking to me again, because I said no to having sex with him and later in the week I refused to tell him my bra size. None of the other boys (or girls) were talking to me either. I didn't want to leave but I didn't know what to do with myself, so I asked the boy who was DJ-ing if I could help him, and he laughed in my face. I went and stood by the door for another minute, and then I went up to my room. Natascha was lying on her bed, reading a book and eating dried apricots.

"Hi," she said.

"Hi," I said.

I climbed up to my bunk and got under the covers. I felt tears coming and turned over to face the wall. I tried not to make any noise. After a minute I heard Natascha get up. She patted me on the back two times, and got back into her bed.

When we returned to school after the trip, we did an exercise where we broke into groups and each group got a big piece of paper with an outline of a boat on it, and we were supposed to put our names in the boat according to our roles in the class. If we thought we were popular we were supposed to write our name in the very middle of the boat, if we were almost popular then close to the middle, and if we were unpopular then far away, at the edge of the boat. I knew I didn't belong in the middle of the boat, but I definitely thought I had moved in from the edge. I thought maybe I was halfway between the middle and the edge. Then we were supposed to talk about how it made us feel to be in our part of the boat. But my group didn't get to that because Benjamin was in it and he and I got into a screaming fight about which one of us was less popular. He said I was at the edge of the boat, I said he was standing on the side of the boat, about to fall off, he said I had already fallen off and was in the water, I said he was farther out in the water, and he said I wasn't even on the piece of paper. I started crying because he was right. The teachers came over and said we could only put our own names in the boat. I left the room and they let me go. I would have taken a bus home, but my bus pass was in my bag in the classroom, so I had to wait until the class finished and go back in for the rest of the day.

In the spring, Natascha's dad had a bike accident. He was riding in the bike lane, and someone opened a car door and he flipped over it. He was in a coma for two weeks, and then he died. Natascha didn't come back to school for a month.

In the meantime, our class was turning a book into a play, and we were going to perform it when we were done. Our homeroom teacher asked for a volunteer to turn Natascha's assigned chapter into a scene, and I raised my hand right away. It had taken me forever to do my own scene in German and it took me forever to do hers, but when I turned it in, no one seemed to care that I did it.

Eventually Natascha came back to school and she didn't talk to anyone. No one tried to talk to her, and no one gave her any trouble. At the end of the year I moved back to the States. My mom and I were really happy to go home, but my dad and my brother had liked it in Germany. Later I found out that Natascha moved away that summer too. I bet everyone in our class missed us a ton.

MY HUMANS

New humans are here. I smell them. Everybody is barking.

I hear them and now I see them.

"Hi," the female says. "You're so quiet."

They go away and they come back.

"She looks like a golden retriever to me," says the female.

I thump my tail.

"Yeah, you're pretty."

I thump my tail some more. The female laughs.

"I thought you wanted a young dog," the male says.

"I don't know. All the other dogs seem so crazy."

The female bends down and puts her fingers through the cage. I taste them.

"She's so sweet," says the female.

"She does seem like a nice dog."

They go away. Eunice comes and opens the door. I wag my tail.

"Here's your big chance, Princess," she says. "Don't blow it."

We are outside and the humans are here. I wag my tail for them.

"Here she is," says Eunice. "We don't know what her name was before, but she just looked like a Princess to me."

"Hi, Princess," the female says. "I'm Jenna and this is Mike."

"I know she's dark for a golden but I think she's a real purebred," says Eunice. "Sometimes they can be reddish like this."

The female kneels down and I lick her whole face. I like the way she tastes. She laughs and scratches me from my head to my tail, under my fur, right on my skin. The male has a ball. He throws it and I fetch it. He laughs and pets me, and I taste his mouth and the inside of his nose.

"Yay!" the female says. "You love her!"

"She's a nice dog," the male says. I wag my tail.

"Sweetheart, huh?" says Eunice.

"Such a sweetheart," says the female.

"She hates it here, she hardly touches her food," says Eunice.

"Yeah, she's skinny," says the male.

"Do you think she was abused?" says the female.

"You never know for sure," says Eunice. "But I don't think so with this one."

"Poor thing," says the female.

"She just said she wasn't abused," says the male.

"She said it was possible," says the female.

She squeezes me.

"So she's six?" says the female.

"My guess is six or seven; that's a great age, they're so calm by then," says Eunice.

"Well, we'll think about it," says the male.

"Oh, baby," says the female. "She needs to get out of the shelter."

"You could go ahead and fill out an application," says Eunice. "That way, if you decide you want her, the paperwork's in, and if you decide you don't, that's okay too."

"Can we just fill it out?" says the female. "Please?"

"Okay," says the male. "We'll fill it out, but we need to talk about this."

I lie down between the female's legs.

"She just adores you," says Eunice.

. . .

Eunice opens the cage.

"Okay, Princess. Time to get your girl parts out."

We go outside. I ride in a truck with other dogs. I sit in a room with other dogs. There are new humans. They look at me and touch me. I feel funny.

Eunice is here. I ride in the truck with the other dogs. We are at the shelter. That female is here. My tail is heavy but I wag it.

The female and Eunice talk about me.

"Good-bye, Princess," says Eunice.

"Thanks for everything," says the female. "Come on, pretty girl. Let's go home and have a bath."

"Oh, no," says Eunice. "No baths for fourteen days because of the stitches."

"Oh," says the female. "Okay."

We are in the car.

We are at a place that smells like dogs and food. I follow the female.

"I guess this is what you were eating at the shelter," she says.

"Do you want a toy?" she says. "Which ones do you like?"

I find a good snack. "Oh, Princess, no," she says. "We have to at least pay for that first."

"My dog already ate part of this," the female says. "Maybe the treats should be kept higher up."

"Maybe," says a human.

"Is beef jerky good for dogs?" says the female.

"I doubt it," says the human.

"Okay, well, this is your first and last piece of jerky, Princess," says the female. "I hope you enjoy it."

I have the snack again. It's delicious.

We are in the car. We get out of the car. I smell everything. We go into a house.

"This is your new home, Princess."

I smell everything in the house.

The male is here. He pets me.

"Wow," he says. "She does not smell good."

"We can't give her a bath for two weeks," says the female.

"Can she live outside until then?" says the male.

"Mike!" says the female.

A pizza is here. I wait to eat it.

"No, Princess, this is people food," says the female.

"So her name is just going to be Princess now? That's it?"

"No, let's talk about it. I just don't know what to call her in the meantime."

"I don't want a dog named Princess."

"Me either, but you don't like any of my ideas."

"If you want to have a dog named Papaya, you can do that on your own. You can take her back to campus with you."

"I never said Papaya, I said Plum."

I wait to eat the pizza.

"I like Red," says the male.

"What about Scarlet or Carmine or some other kind of red? That's why I thought Plum, it's kind of a red."

"Those all sound like celebrity baby names."

"No they don't. What celebrity named their baby one of those names?"

"You tell me, you're the one who knows all that stuff."

The female puts a bowl of kibble on the floor. I sniff it and knock it over.

"Princess!" says the female. "That's your dinner."

Later the female puts a blanket down and says, "This is where Princess sleeps." The humans are on the other side of the door.

The doorbell rings and Jenna leaves. She is back with a box. I smell it and she opens it. "This is your new dog bed!" she says.

There is a bed and I lie on it.

"Do you love it?" says Jenna. I thump my tail.

She scratches me all over my body. I lean into the scratches, wherever they are.

I smell meat. It's on the counter. Jenna and the male are talking about the meat. I am waiting.

"That's what dogs are naturally supposed to eat."

"Really? Does it cost six dollars a day in the wild?"

"She suffered so much before we got her, she should at least eat good food."

"She didn't suffer! Eunice said she was fine. And eating kibble is not suffering."

"She obviously does not like that food, Mike!"

"I'm not feeding her this when you go back to school."

"Fine, give her cancer. I'm not making dinner."

"Fine, neither am I."

"Fine. Why don't you order one of your magical buffalo chicken pizzas?"

"Maybe I will."

The meat is in my bowl. I eat it. It is delicious.

"Look how much she likes it," says Jenna.

I am wet. I try to escape. Mike gives me snacks. Jenna covers me with water. I try to escape.

I am in the bedroom.

"But she smells good now," says Jenna.

"She can smell good in the hallway," says Mike.

"She's lonely," says Jenna.

"Dogs can't be lonely," says Mike.

"Of course they can, they're pack animals," says Jenna. "She wants to be near us so bad that she's lying on the cold, hard floor."

"It's ninety degrees out and she's lying on like two inches of her own hair."

"It's my last night with you guys for five days."

"And you want to spend it with the dog," says Mike. "Clearly you're going to do what you want, so just go get it."

"I love you, baby," she says.

The dog bed is in the room. I lie on it.

They are moving in the human bed. I stand up to see. They are licking each other. They are moving around. It smells good.

Mike looks at me.

"The dog is watching us," he says.

"So?" says Jenna.

"I can't concentrate."

"Princess, lie down," says Jenna. I lie down.

There are many good smells.

Mike puts his feet on the floor and I lick them. They taste delicious.

"Ugh," says Mike. He leaves and comes back and Jenna leaves and comes back. She scratches behind my ears.

· · ·

Jenna is not here. There is kibble in my bowl. I knock it over.

I am in the dog bed and Mike is in the human bed.

He pets me.

"Here I am with you," says Mike. "And Jenna is back at school. With Nick. So that's great."

Jenna is not here. There is kibble in my bowl. I knock it over.

Jenna is not here. Mike puts kibble in my bowl. I knock it over.

"Fuck this shit," he says. He puts meat in my bowl. I try to eat it. It's very hard and cold.

"Yeah, go ahead and eat it frozen," says Mike. "That's six frozen dollars right there."

Jenna is here. She is crying.

"Come on, baby," says Mike. "It was supposed to be funny."

"There should have been some kind of warning that the dog was going to die," says Jenna.

"Are you getting your period, by any chance?"

"That should be, like, part of the rating. D for death of dog."

"Are you?"

"None of your business," says Jenna.

"Called it," says Mike.

Jenna sits on Mike. I get on the couch.

"Off," says Mike.

"Aw," says Jenna. "She wants to comfort me."

I follow them to the bedroom and I get on the bed.

"Absolutely not," says Mike.

"Princess, off," says Jenna.

I move to a different part of the bed. The bed has many smells and they are all good.

"Oh baby, please?" says Jenna.

"This is not fair," says Mike. "You two are taking advantage of the situation."

"Just for tonight," says Jenna.

"Ugh," says Mike.

I sleep in the bed with the humans.

I find a very good snack.

I don't feel my best.

I am in the bed with the humans. I wake up and stand up. Mike wakes up and holds me over the edge of the bed. I throw up. I feel better. Mike turns on the light.

"Jenna, wake up," he says.

She wakes up.

"The dog threw up, and I think there's blood in it."

She sits up. "Mm," she says. "That's a tampon." She lies back down.

"Oh my god," says Mike.

"I'll clean it up," says Jenna. "Will you take her out?"

Mike gets out of bed and says, "Come on, dog."

I see a good snack and eat it.

We are outside and then we are inside. The mess is there and I wonder if I should clean it up.

"The tampon is missing," says Jenna.

"What?" says Mike.

"It's not here anymore. Was she right behind you the whole time?"

"I think so," he says. "Maybe not. Oh god."

"I'm calling the vet," says Jenna.

"You're a disgusting animal," says Mike.

Mike and I lie in the bed together.

Jenna comes back.

"They want us to bring her in so they can surgically remove it," she says.

"How much is that going to cost?" says Mike.

"I don't know, a lot."

"Can't we just make her throw it up?"

"They said not to, she might choke."

"She threw it up once, she can throw it up again."

"Oh god," says Jenna. She cleans up the mess.

We are in the bathroom. I drink something.

"I can't believe she just drank it," says Jenna.

"She eats garbage," says Mike. "What do you expect?"

I throw up. The snack is here again but Jenna takes it away.

We are in bed.

"That was a very bad thing you did, Princess," says Jenna.

"Her name is going to be Princess forever," says Mike. "Fuck."

"I wish you didn't have to go back to campus," says Mike.

"I'll be back on Friday."

"And I have to stay here with this disgusting dog."

"Oh please, you love her."

"And you're on campus with Nick."

"What?" says Jenna. "Are you being serious right now? You cannot even tell me that you're still worried about Nick."

"I just wish he wasn't on campus with you."

"Seriously? Do you not trust me at all?"

"I do trust you. I just don't like it. I don't like him."

"Babe. Come on. This is crazy. I'm here with you. I chose you."

"I know."

"We have a dog together."

"I noticed."

"She's like our first kid."

"I hope our real kids are better."

"We'll get through this year," says Jenna. "Less than a year. Eight months. And then we have the rest of our lives."

"Okay," says Mike.

"I love you," says Jenna.

"I love you too," says Mike.

"You know what I want tonight?" says Jenna.

"What?"

"Butt sex."

Mike laughs. "Why wait until tonight?"

Mike chases Jenna and I chase Mike.

We are in the bedroom.

"Princess, stay on the floor," says Mike.

I get on the bed.

"Fuck, Princess, no," says Mike.

"Just leave her," says Jenna. "Come on."

I am close to Mike and Jenna. There is a new smell and it's an incredibly good smell.

"I can come stay on campus with you," says Mike.

"What about Princess?" says Jenna. I wag my tail.

"I'll bring her."

"Babe, I just kind of need a weekend to myself."

"What do you need to do?"

"Go to Halloween parties, I don't know."

"What if Nick is there?"

"Oh my god! Are we going to talk about this for the rest of our lives?"

"Just answer the question. What if he's there?"

"We still have a lot of the same friends, I can't help it if I run into him."

"But you don't have to go to a party with him."

"I'm not going to a party with him!"

"If you went to a party and he was there, would you leave?"

"I don't know," says Jenna.

"If he's there will you text me? Just so I know he's there?"

"I'm not going to do that! This is crazy. We're just friends."

"Wait, now you're friends? You can't be friends."

"You can't tell me who I can and cannot be friends with, Michael."

"Yes I can, when it comes to Nick I can."

Mike and I walk. I wait outside. We walk and I wait outside. We have food.

"Don't tell Jenna about our little Halloween party," says Mike. "If she's allowed to drink beer, I'm allowed to drink beer. But she can never know about Blessings II Go, Blessings II Go is not allowed."

We are home. We eat the food.

"This chicken doesn't taste like roadkill to you, does it?" says Mike. "You think Jenna is the best. She is the best but she's not right about everything. She's wrong about this chicken and she's wrong about Nick. She's wrong about my beer belly. You like my beer belly, right, girl? You think that's why Jenna didn't want me to come to the party? I'm too fat to be Tarzan now?"

"I should go to campus," says Mike. "I'm not too drunk to drive."

We are sitting.

"Maybe I'm a little too drunk," says Mike. "Jenna was going to be a smokin' Jane. I don't know who you were going to be. Maybe you were going to be Phil Collins. 'Cause you'll be in my heart, yes you'll be in my heart.' Fucking Disney ruins everything."

"I could still go. I could go find them and Nick would be pumping the keg for her like how he's so fucking romantic and I could swing in and pick up the keg and smash it over his head. I would wear a wig and a loincloth and everything."

"What a fucking asshole, that guy. You would think he

was an asshole if you met him. You would smell it from a mile away. Smelling like a giant fucking asshole."

"Sorry, girl, this might be the beer talking. Or maybe that chicken. That chicken is probably not the best. I don't trust that guy at all. But I do trust Jenna, I trust Jenna."

Mike is drinking. I am licking my vagina and my butt.

"She's done with him," says Mike. "She's been done with him. She promised she's done with him."

"You know what you should not do? You should not be the other dog. You should not fuck a boy dog who already has a girl dog. And if that boy dog says he's going to break up with his girl dog for you, don't do it. It's never gonna fucking work. Just kidding, it's different for dogs. You can fuck any dog you want and they can fuck any dog they want. Except not you because your vagina doesn't work anymore. Well it works but you know what I mean. There's no point."

"She should have picked me to begin with. He told her he loved her when she told him about me. For the first time ever. You think that's a coincidence, girl?"

I thump my tail.

"Robbie was like, don't get a dog, man. He said his sister got a dog with her girlfriend and they made a deal that if they broke up, whoever got broken up with would get the dog. So the sister tried to make the girlfriend dump her, and the girlfriend tried to make the sister dump her.

And in the end Robbie's sister lost the dog and her heart was broken forever."

"Whatever. Robbie never liked Jenna."

Later I am in the human part of the bed. Mike's arms are around me. There are noises and good smells inside of Mike. He goes to the bathroom. He is back.

"Ugh," he says. "You don't think that meat really is roadkill, do you, girl?"

He leaves and comes back and leaves and comes back. He squeezes me.

I am still in Mike's arms.

Jenna is here. She licks Mike a lot. She squeezes me a lot. She smells different.

"Hi baby," says Mike. "I missed you."

"I missed you too," says Jenna. "I'm sorry I made you worry. I just wanted a weekend with my friends."

"I know, I'm sorry," he says. "I was being a jerk. I was being a little crazy."

"A little," says Jenna. "But I love you anyway."

Later I am on my side of the bed. Jenna comes in.

"Princess!" she says. "You're in my spot. You sleep at the end of the bed."

I have to move to the end of the bed.

· · ·

I sleep at the end of the bed every night.

"Princess," says Mike. "I have to tell you a big secret."

We have a buffalo chicken pizza and beer.

"I'm going to ask your mom to marry me. At gradua-tion."

"Princess," says Mike. "Forget what I said yesterday."

We have a buffalo chicken pizza and beer.

"Casey says it's not a good idea. She says it's Jenna's spe-cial day. And she says I need to wait until I know Jenna is the one. Obviously Jenna is the one. You and I both know Jenna is the one. Jenna is the one for us."

We are in a place with a lot of humans.

Jenna is here and she squeezes me. I am carrying some-thing important on my neck.

"What is this?" she says.

"Open it," says Mike.

"Oh my god," says Jenna. "What is happening right now?"

"Oh," says Jenna. "Earrings."

"Congratulations, baby," says Mike. "Do you like them?"

"Do I not deserve white pearls?" says Jenna.

"What?" says Mike. "No, I just thought you would like these because they're different."

"No, then I love them," she says.

I am at school. There are other dogs and other humans and a human named Mo.

Mo says, "Jump," and I jump. She gives me a snack.

Mo says, "Through the tunnel," and I go through the tunnel. She gives me a snack.

"You are a VERY smart dog," says Mo. She gives me a snack.

"I know Mo seems crazy but I think she's really good," says Jenna. "You handle Princess tomorrow and you'll see."

"I think we could have saved a hundred and forty bucks," Mike says. "I could do the same things she does. And Princess is perfect already."

"She eats trash," says Jenna.

"It's not like she's going to stop because she can jump over a chair and crawl through a tunnel."

Mike makes ice cream.

I follow him and the ice cream to the living room. Mike licks Jenna.

"What do you want to watch?" she says.

"You pick," he says. "Oh my god, guess what? I ran into Robbie in the city today."

"Oh my god!" says Jenna. "What was he doing there?"

"He had a job interview at a high school. He was wearing a suit and tie."

"No shit. How is he doing?"

"Good, I think."

"That's so crazy you just ran into each other."

"I know. You know what he asked me?" Mike says. "He asked me if you were still cheating on me." Mike laughs.

"What?" says Jenna.

"Isn't that funny?" says Mike.

"Uh," says Jenna.

"Come on babe, he hasn't seen us in a long time. Baby, what's wrong? It's not a big deal."

I wait for ice cream.

"You would have told me if anything happened last year, right?" says Mike. "If you kissed Nick or something?"

Jenna starts to cry.

"Oh my god," says Mike.

Jenna cries a lot. Mike moves to another part of the couch. I get on the couch between them.

"You kissed him?" says Mike.

Jenna looks at Mike. I look at Mike.

"You fucked him?" says Mike. "Oh my god, you fucked him." He stands up. I get off the couch. Jenna cries.

I follow Mike to the bedroom. Jenna follows us.

"Please," she says, "please don't leave."

He lies down. I lick him. He doesn't move. I lick him again.

I go to the living room and eat the ice cream. I go back to the bedroom. Mike and Jenna are on the bed. They are both feeling bad. I get on the bed and lie down at the end.

"I think it was only twice," says Jenna. "I stopped. I didn't want to cheat on you."

"That's so sweet of you."

"Please, Mikey. Please don't do this. It was such a long time ago. It was such a stupid mistake."

"Oh, well, if it was a long time ago and if it was a mistake."

"Please, baby."

"I'm taking Princess out."

I get off the bed.

"Okay," says Jenna. "Do you want me to come?"

"No," says Mike.

I follow him to the living room. He puts my leash on. He goes back to the bedroom and I follow him.

"Did you fuck him on Halloween?"

Jenna starts crying. She goes under the covers.

"I knew it," says Mike.

I follow him to the living room. We go outside and walk and walk.

We are home and Jenna is walking in the house. Mike and I get into bed.

Jenna gets into bed and takes her clothes off.

Mike jumps up.

"Fuck you," he says. "Put your clothes back on."

Jenna cries. Mike leaves. Jenna puts her clothes on. Mike comes back and gets into the bed.

"I'm sorry," says Jenna. She is crying. "Thank you for sleeping in here with me. I think I would die if you didn't."

There is a space between Mike and Jenna and I sleep in it.

"You should probably get out of here for a couple of days," says Mike.

"Where should I go?" says Jenna.

"How could you move in here with me?" says Mike.

"I'll call my mom," says Jenna. "Do you want me to take Princess with me?"

"It's better for her if she stays here," says Mike. "She has obedience school."

Jenna leaves.

Mike and I are in the car.

We are at school.

"Down," says Mike. I lie down. I get a snack.

"Stay," says Mike. I stay. I get a snack.

"Down." Snack. "Stay." Snack. "Down." Snack. "Stay." Snack. "Down." Snack. "Stay." Snack. "Down." Snack.

"Stay." Snack. "Down." Snack. "Stay." Snack. "Down." Snack. "Stay." Snack. "Down." Snack. "Stay." Snack.

"Okay, folks," says Mo. "Before we leave, the tip of the day. This is for all of you whose dogs steal food. You make yourself a hamburger and put it down in the living room and you realize you forgot your beer and you go back to the kitchen and get it. When you come back, the hamburger is gone and your dog is licking his chops. If that happens to you, here's what you do. You roll up a newspaper and you hit yourself in the head with it. Don't be a moron and leave your hamburger alone with your dog. Because your dog is going to eat the hamburger."

Mike and I are in the car.

"You know who's a fucking hamburger?" says Mike. "Jenna is the fucking hamburger. I left her on the coffee table and Nick fucking ate her."

"Or maybe Nick is the hamburger and she ate him. I don't fucking know. I don't know which is worse."

Mike and I are in the car. I am next to Mike.

We have hot dogs. I eat one.

"Jenna says that's like a person eating half a dozen donuts. Ha."

We ride and ride. Mike opens the windows and I smell a million smells.

We are at a new house. "This is your aunt Casey and

your uncle Luis," says Mike. Casey makes noises. Uncle Luis has hot dogs and I eat one. There is a small human girl named Patsy and a small human boy named T-Rex. They smell better than other humans.

Patsy brushes me. "Pretty pretty Princess," she says.

"I thought she was my fucking Luis," says Mike.

"Language," says Casey. "But you'll find another Luis. One who isn't a lying, cheating whore."

"She's not a whore," says Mike. "Don't call her that."

T-Rex has many snacks. We eat them together. "This is a Teddy Graham," he says, "this is a banana, this is blubbery yogurt, this is a Starburst."

"Aren't you glad you didn't ask her to marry you?" says Casey.

"Maybe," says Mike. "I don't know."

Casey makes a noise. "God, I'm so allergic to her."

"I know," says Mike, "I'm sorry. We'll leave tomorrow. I was just going crazy there."

"I know," says Casey. "It's okay."

I sleep in a new bed with Mike.

We are home. Jenna is here. She is sad.

Mike and I are not sad. I wag my tail.

"I want to try to work it out," says Mike.

"Oh my god," says Jenna. She squeezes Mike.

We are in bed. Mike and Jenna move around. I close my eyes.

"I'm sorry, I can't," says Mike.

I get up and move to the space between them.

I sleep between the humans every night.

Jenna is gone. I am in the bed with Mike. His arms are around me. He squeezes me and unsqueezes me. I sigh a deep sigh and close my eyes.

JERKS

When I got into grad school, my boyfriend told me that we were at a crossroads and we needed to take stock of our relationship and decide whether to continue together or separately. While I tried to think of what to say, he explained that his vote was for separately.

I quit my job and moved back to Massachusetts. I moved into my old bedroom at my dad's house because I didn't have time to find a summer job or a sublet. My dad felt bad for me and gave me a talk about how this was an opportunity to center myself. He said he would pay my expenses until I left for school in August, which was really nice and kind of depressing.

The expenses he covered were: the minimum payment on my student loan bills, a monthly membership to a darkroom, unlimited film, and whatever I needed from the grocery store. What I wanted most from the grocery store was ice cream, but it turned out a person could not "need" sweets, or magazines, or makeup. I also wanted to buy breakup underwear, but I assumed that was not a need either.

I wasn't really thinking about when I was going to need the breakup underwear, but I wanted to have it on hand. Then the second week I was home, I went to the art supply store and ran into the boy I loved in high school, Silas. I wasn't supposed to love him because my friend Kat loved him, so I loved him from far away like all of the other art girls and drama girls and drug girls. He was beautiful and brooding and he loved none of us back.

I did get to hang out with Silas a couple of times in high school, but I didn't think he knew who I was. Once, I went with Kat and two of our other friends to get weed from him, which was just an excuse for Kat to see him. Silas's parents were out, and we stayed to smoke with him and two of his friends. Silas and Kat coupled up right away and the other guys checked us out. One chose one of my friends, and the other chose the other. I was pretty sure none of them even saw me there, especially not Silas.

But when I saw him at the art store he said, "Deaf Girl!" and then, "Oh shit, I'm sorry."

"It's fine," I said. "It's Jane." Deaf Girl was my behind-the-back nickname in high school, even though I could hear fine with my hearing aids.

Silas was working in the framing department and I needed mats cut. He hadn't aged especially well—it looked like maybe he had moved on to harder drugs before eventually cleaning up—but my heart beat faster anyway. He seemed like he was doing fine now. I wondered if he thought I was doing fine. I hoped I looked like I was doing awesome.

Silas cut my mats for free and said it was about to be his lunch break, and asked if I wanted to get burritos across the street. I didn't have any cash, but he said it was his treat. We didn't have a lot to say to each other and I was preoccupied by my bare legs sticking to the booth, but my heart didn't stop its beating and I agreed to go to a party with him later that week.

When we had sex it was urgent. He held my hand at the party and started sucking on my fingers in the car, and by the time we got upstairs to his apartment I was hotter and wetter than I had ever been. Later I wondered if it was the kind of sex you could only have if you had been waiting for it since high school. Obviously Silas hadn't been waiting for it since high school, but he knew how to make it seem like he had been.

I started going to Silas's apartment almost every night. He only had a couch, a TV, and a bed, but it was clean and

I liked it there. I couldn't explain it, but all I wanted to
do was be in his bed and let him do whatever he wanted
to me. Maybe I could have explained it through the high
school crush, or through the getting dumped, but it seemed
like it was more, or maybe less, than that. Like a purely and
exceptionally physical thing.

In July my dad's girlfriend asked me if I wanted to babysit
for her coworker's kid. I didn't. I had promised myself I
would never babysit again, three separate times: once when
I graduated from high school, once when I graduated from
college, and then again three months after that, after I
spent the summer babysitting. I meant it every time, but
I really meant it the last time. At the end of that summer I
had a meeting with myself and told myself it was time to
be an adult.

And now it was almost two years after that last promise, and I had spent the past eight weeks living at home,
asking my dad for cash and having him ask me if all the
time I was spending at Silas's apartment was really helping
me center myself. So it was hard to turn down the babysitting job.

And when I hesitated, my dad's girlfriend smacked her
forehead and said, "Oh my god, I can't believe I forgot!
The kid is hearing impaired!"

"Oh," I said. "Great." I still didn't want to do it but I

wondered if that meant I should. It did seem like a big coincidence, and my dad's girlfriend seemed to think it was some kind of fate. Maybe I was supposed to meet the kid and be his hearing-impaired role model or something. Show him that I turned out fine, awesome. If that was the case, I guessed the babysitting wouldn't kill me.

That weekend I went to meet them. The mom, Susanna, let me in, and said the kid was still sleeping. There didn't seem to be a dad there. The mom was older than I expected, maybe mid-forties, and she wasn't unpretty but she looked kind of spent. Their apartment was the first floor of a small house. She led me through the hall and the kitchen and out to the back porch. She brought me a glass of water.

"I can't believe you're hearing impaired," she said. "I wouldn't have known on the phone."

"I do pretty well," I said.

"Your speech is almost totally normal," she said.

"Thanks," I said.

"Timmy and I are so excited to have a hearing-impaired babysitter."

I didn't say anything.

"So, you're just in the area for the summer?"

"Yeah, I'm going back to school in the fall."

She didn't ask for what, and I didn't tell her. Whenever I tell people I take pictures, they say they do too, and want to show me the same picture that everybody has of whatever bridge in Venice. Either that or they try to hire me for their sister's stepkid's wedding, and I have to explain that I don't do weddings, like I'm too good for them or something. I actually think I'm not good enough for weddings—there are too many people, and everything happens so fast.

Susanna told me the kid's whole story—he was born completely deaf, and they didn't think he would ever hear or speak. The doctors said the cochlear implant was their only chance, so they got on the waiting list for the surgery, and when he was two they got a call that someone had canceled and they could have the spot if they brought him in the next day. He got the implant, and now he was eight and doing well. He went to a regular school where his teachers wore microphones that fed into his device, and he went to speech therapy. Susanna said he was easy to understand once you knew him, but she was hoping his speech would get better with the therapy. She went in and got his device to show me. It magnetically attached to his implant, which was under his skin.

Then she asked if I had always been hearing impaired and I gave her my deaf history. My parents realized something was wrong when I started answering the phone, and I would hold it up to my right ear and immediately switch it to my left ear. We went to a million hearing doctors but no one could diagnose me. Finally they took me to Boston, to the fanciest ear doctor. He said that some tubes in my ears were bigger than they were supposed to be. I had most of my hearing in my left ear, but was legally deaf in my right ear. I got hearing aids, and when I was a teenager the doctors wanted me to try an implant. Not a cochlear implant but a bone-anchored hearing aid, which was what it sounded like—a hearing aid that snapped on to a screw that was anchored in the skull. I didn't tell Susanna or anybody else that when I imagined the screw in my skull and the snapping and unsnapping, I felt a charge run through all of my bones. I stuck with the regular hearing aids, and now I had fancy ones that were wireless.

Then the kid came out to the porch. He was only wearing underwear, and when he saw me he turned around and went back inside. He came back out with a T-shirt on, but still no pants. He didn't look at me. He was scowling, but he had a sweet face under his long blond hair. His mom grabbed his hand and said, "This is Jane." He looked at me for a second.

"This is Timmy," she said to me. She offered him his hearing aids but he shook his head.

"Maybe show him yours?" she said.

I removed my hearing aids and held them out to him, but he didn't look at them or at me. He went out to the backyard.

"Oh well," Susanna said. "Maybe later."

We watched him walk around the backyard and look at things, and Susanna tried to introduce me to him one more time, by yelling at him from the porch. I thought he was straight-up deaf without the hearing aids attached to his implant. Maybe he wasn't. But in my experience, hearing people never really believed that you couldn't hear them, even or maybe especially if they were your parents. Either way, there was no response from Timmy.

"He's just shy," said Susanna.

"No problem," I said.

On the way out she asked me what my rate was, and I told her I made eighteen at my last babysitting job. She looked surprised and said she paid twelve, which she thought was pretty generous for one kid. She looked like she was doing the best she could, and I didn't have any other job offers, so I said twelve was okay.

When I picked Timmy up from summer school later that week he seemed perfectly happy to leave with me. I asked him if he remembered me and he said yes. His speech wasn't that different from any other eight-year-old boy's. I asked him about his day, and he said it was fine. He didn't do anything fun and he didn't have a favorite subject. When we got to the apartment he let us in with the key in his backpack. I followed him into the dining room and was kind of shocked at how much of a mess it was. The table was covered with papers, and the floor was covered with more papers and magazines and toys. Next to the dining room was the living room, which I also hadn't seen on Saturday, and it was even worse. The toys spilled over from the dining room, the couch cushions were on the floor, and in the window one side of the curtain rod had fallen and the curtain was bunched up on the lower end. In the dining room, Timmy had made a beeline for a laptop on the table and was sitting on top of a pile of clothes in a chair.

"Are you allowed to use that computer?" I said.

"Yes," said Timmy. "Of course I am."

"Okay," I said. "I'm just going to check with your mom."

I texted her, and she texted back saying it was okay but he needed to do his homework first. I asked what his homework was, and she said he would know and he would tell me.

"Okay, Timmy," I said. "Your mom says you can use the computer but you have to do your homework first."

"No!" he said.

"What's your homework?" I said.

"I don't know!" He continued playing.

I reached toward the computer, but Timmy slammed it shut before I touched it. He ran into the living room and threw himself onto the cushionless couch.

"I hate you!" he yelled. "You're a jerk!"

"You can't talk to me like that," I said.

He turned the TV on.

"Timmy. Turn it off."

"I hate you!" he yelled.

He alternated between telling me that he hated me and calling me a jerk for the next hour. I got him to turn off the TV but he wouldn't move from the couch. For a while

I sat in the dining room, getting a headache from the yelling, and wondering when he was going to wear himself out. Finally I made him a snack of peanut butter on crackers and brought it to him. He was quiet when he was eating, and I took the opportunity to suggest that when he was done we could start his homework. He told me I was a big jerk, but when he was done he came back into the dining room and sat down and opened his math book. He completed one page and said, "That's enough." I texted his mom again, and she texted back that the assignment sheet was on the table. I went through the piles of papers until I found it. I told him he had to do two pages of math and four pages of his reading workbook and he said, "See, I told you you were wrong." But he did the pages, and when he was done he called me a jerk again and we went to the playground.

When we got there he ran around like crazy. I offered to play with him but he didn't want to play with me or any of the kids there. I sat on a bench with some moms and watched kids trip in a poorly placed water drainage ditch between the bench area and the rest of the playground. After half an hour Timmy came running up and said he needed to go to the bathroom. There were Porta-Pottys right there, but he insisted that we drive home. When we got there we couldn't get in. Somehow the key didn't work anymore. I tried every lock trick I knew, but I couldn't get the door open.

Timmy called me a stupid jerk and tried the lock himself. Then he said he didn't need to use the bathroom anymore. He clearly did, so we drove to a pizza place, and then back to the playground. I texted Susanna to tell her we had locked ourselves out, and she said she would meet us at the playground.

I watched Timmy play on a big round wheel. Other kids were sitting on top of it, and he was pushing it and then jumping onto it himself. It seemed dangerous but I was too exhausted to do anything about it, and if I had learned anything in my years of babysitting, it was that nothing was as dangerous as it seemed to me. All the times my heart had stopped had always been for nothing.

So I watched him push the wheel with his strange intensity. He didn't even seem to notice the other kids, and I wondered if he had a bigger problem than being deaf. I wondered if I could just tell Susanna that I wasn't coming back tomorrow. I had never done anything like that, but I had also never been called a jerk for an entire afternoon. And it was becoming increasingly apparent that there was going to be no deaf mentor–deaf mentee relationship. Timmy was much deafer than I was, he was doing much better than I had, and he was a little asshole.

Finally Susanna got there and I walked out to meet her.

"How was everything?" she said.

"Good," I said. "We had a pretty hard time with the homework."

"It'll get better," she said. "He needs to get used to you."

"I know," I said, "but I was thinking that this might not be the best fit. By the time he gets used to me I'll have to leave."

"He'll be fine," she said. She started getting red.

"He was really upset with me," I said. "Maybe it would be better if you looked for someone else."

"Excuse me," a woman called from the playground, "is this your daughter?" She was holding the hand of a little girl who was sobbing.

"No!" Susanna snapped. "I don't even have a daughter!"

She turned back to me. "Well, we'll see you tomorrow."

"Okay," I said. My heart was thumping. I went to my car and pulled out of the parking lot. I realized she hadn't paid me, and if I wanted any money at all, I would have to go back. On the way home Silas called and I ended up going to his apartment. I didn't want to because I was tired and in a bad mood, but he said he would take care of me, and he did. He made me a double-decker peanut butter and banana sandwich for dinner, and asked me what happened. I didn't feel like talking about it, so I just told him that I hated babysitting and I was going to quit. When we were done eating he came around behind me and took out my hearing aids and started rubbing my head and my neck. He couldn't have known that wearing the hearing aids made me tired, but it did. He rubbed my

head and my neck and the day started to go away, and
then he took off my shirt and unhooked my bra.

The next day on the way to Timmy's school, I made a plan.
As soon as I picked him up I was going to tell him the
schedule for the day, and I was going to get him to agree to
it. He clearly needed structure. I had also brought a camera, my two and a quarter camera, thinking at worst I could
distract him with it, and at best I could take some pictures.

Timmy didn't seem unhappy to see me, and I wondered
if he had forgotten I was a jerk and if the day would be fine
after all. We drove to speech therapy, and when we got
there we had half an hour to kill. We went to a grocery
store to get a snack, and Timmy somehow disappeared in
the aisles. I tried to call his name in a calm voice, and finally
I found him holding two half gallons of chocolate milk. I
helped him put them back and I paid for our apples and
waters and we left. Timmy wanted to eat in the graveyard
across the street. I wanted to say no but I couldn't think of
a reason why not, other than that I didn't want to. He saw
me thinking and said, "My other babysitter takes me."

"Fine," I said.

We ate on a bench and then walked around and read
the grave markers. It seemed like he really had been there
before, because he had favorite graves.

"Look." He brought me to three graves, one little and two big. "This one was a baby. And this is her mom and dad. The dad lived to be ninety-nine."

"Wow," I said.

"Yeah," he said. "Wow."

"You know what you could do?" I said. I took a piece of paper and a pencil out of his backpack and showed him how to rub over the letters to copy them to the paper.

"Isn't that cool?"

"No," he said. "I don't want to do that."

"Okay," I said.

When we got to speech, the therapist offered for me to come in, and said that Timmy's other babysitters did, so they could help him at home. I explained that I was only going to be babysitting for a short time. I sat and read magazines in the waiting room. Susanna texted me to see if I could stay later. She said a work thing came up, and she would be so, so grateful if I could stay until nine thirty or ten. Bedtime would be easy, Timmy was good at it. I couldn't decide what to do. It would ruin my plan to go straight to Silas's to get fucked, but I was bad at saying no. Finally I texted her that I could stay but I had made plans to meet my boyfriend at eight thirty, and could he come hang out at their apartment with me. It felt wrong to say boyfriend, but I couldn't really call him my rebound, or my animal sex.

Susanna wrote back that it was fine, and thank you so

much. When speech therapy was over I drove Timmy home, and on the way I reminded him that he was going to have to do homework first thing.

"I know," he said. "And then can I watch one show and then can we go to the playground again?"

"Sure," I said. I was starting to feel bad about the day before. Now I thought that Timmy wasn't so much of an asshole as a really stressed-out little kid. I could have done a better job with him if I'd been more prepared. But Susanna should have prepared me. Maybe she didn't know to. Or maybe she decided not to, because there was no way I would have taken the job if she had.

Timmy did his homework peacefully and I warmed up his dinner and let him eat it in front of the TV. He sat on the floor with his face inches from the screen, and I wondered if that was just a bad habit, or if he could hear better that way. When I was a kid I could barely hear the TV, and then I got hearing aids and could hear more of it, and then I found out about closed captions and wondered why no one had ever mentioned or offered them before. It was amazing to read every word that everyone said.

"Do you ever watch with closed captions?" I said. "The words on the bottom of the screen?"

"I just like to listen," he said.

I realized he probably couldn't read fast enough for the captions, anyway.

I got my camera and took a picture of Timmy in front

of the TV. The bottom left quarter of the frame was Timmy's face and the bottom right quarter was the glowing TV, with only a thin line in between.

"Hey!" He whipped around when the shutter went off. I was surprised he heard it. He studied me and the camera and said, "Oh. That's a big camera."

"All cameras used to be this big," I said. "Do you want to look through it? It makes square pictures."

But he had already turned back to the TV. When the show ended we drove to the playground, and I let him play until the sun started to go down. On the way home we stopped to get ice cream, and in exchange I made Timmy promise that he was going to get right in the bath and then right into bed.

He did get right in the bath. He took his hearing aids off while I ran it for him, and then he got in and played. I waited for him to use soap and shampoo, and when he didn't I realized I was going to have to write him a note. I went and got some paper and a marker and wrote WASH YOUR HAIR AND WASH EVERYWHERE WITH SOAP.

"Wash, your, hair, and, wash, every, where, with, soap," he read, but he didn't start washing anything.

He took the sign from me and submerged it in the water. He held it up. I rolled my eyes at him and held out my finger to say, "Wait." I went and got my camera and he held the dripping sign in front of his face. I took the picture from the other side of the bathroom, with the whole tub and bar and shower curtain, and Timmy's small wet chest and the bleeding letters.

I took the sign from him and threw it in the garbage. He grinned. I waited thirty seconds and wrote him a new note: HURRY UP!

I thought he was going to get mad but he read the words out loud again and smiled a goofy smile.

I poured him shampoo but he did nothing with it, so I scooped it out of his hand and washed his hair.

"Mm," he said, leaning into my fingertips.

I rubbed his head a little longer and then rinsed his hair. I put a bar of soap in his hands and made washing motions under my arms and over my crotch. He thought this was hilarious.

I underlined HURRY UP! twice, and finally he washed himself. I got him out and dried his hair well and brought him his hearing aids. He put them on.

"Where are your pajamas?" I said.

"In my closet," he said.

"Can you get them?" I said.

He went into his room and came out five seconds later. "I can't see in there," he said.

"Let's turn on the light," I said.

"It's broken," he said.

"Okay," I said. "I'll go in." I used my phone to light the way. I tried not to step on anything as I made my way to the closet, but it was impossible. The floor was covered with dark heaps of toys, books, and clothes. So was the bed, and I wondered if he ever slept there. In the closet I found hanging shelves with exactly one T-shirt and one pair of underwear on them, so I took those things and made my way back out.

Timmy put on the clothes and got into his mom's bed. "Can we read books?" he said.

"One quick book," I said.

He picked one out and I lay down next to him and read it. When I was done he handed me his hearing aids and asked me to tuck him in. I tucked him in and he closed his eyes. I took a picture of him, tiny and human at the top of the frame, with his hearing aids on the table next to him, and the rest of the picture the smooth white sheet. I turned out the light.

"Leave the door open!" he said, so I did.

I cleaned up the bathroom and put the wet sign and the dry sign in a plastic bag and in my backpack. I didn't want his mom to find them, like I shouldn't have had to write him notes in the bathtub or something. Then I took a few more pictures. I found a flashlight on the shelf in the kitchen and shone it into Timmy's bedroom and took a picture. Then I took a picture of the contents of the fridge, which was full of what I guessed were mostly very old leftovers in take-out containers. There was no fresh juice or milk or anything. Finally I took a picture of the windows in the living room with the fallen curtain rod, and then sat down on the couch. I doubted that Susanna would want me to use the pictures of the apartment, but I wondered if she would really be able to prove it was her house. She would probably let me use the pictures of Timmy, because parents loved it when I took pictures of their kids. But the pictures of Timmy weren't exactly portraits, and I wanted them in conjunction with the pictures of the apartment. I wondered if I could get a picture of Susanna, looking like she did when I first met her, maybe yelling to Timmy from the porch, or maybe lying next to him on top of the white sheet, sleeping. If I kept baby-sitting and I got them to like me, I could shoot a whole essay.

Silas got there and I let him in. He put his bike in the hallway and I gave him a tour. I used the flashlight to show him Timmy's room.

"Whoa," said Silas. "Is the kid in there somewhere?"

"Oh my god," I said. "No." I showed him Timmy in his mom's bedroom. He was fast asleep.

"He doesn't look so bad," he said.

"He's not," I said.

"Can he hear us?" he said.

"Nope," I said. "We could scream at the top of our lungs and he wouldn't hear us."

"Cool," he said. "Is there any food?"

I showed him the inside of the fridge and he said, "That's disgusting."

We went back to the living room and sat on the couch. Silas started kissing my neck and I made him stop and turned on the TV. In all my years of babysitting I had never had a boy over to make out with after the kids were asleep, and now that I had the perfect candidate I didn't even want to. I just wanted to go home.

We watched TV until we heard a car pull in. I gathered up my stuff and went to meet Susanna at the door.

"Hi," she said. "How was it today?"

"Much better," I said.

"Oh good," she said.

She checked on Timmy and then came and stood in the doorway to the living room.

"This is Silas," I said.

They said hi.

Susanna counted out the money for the two days and paid me. "It's a few dollars short but I'll pay you the rest next week."

"Okay," I said.

"So we'll see you then?"

"Yup," I said. "Unless you do find someone else."

"Why would I find someone else?"

"Well, I mean, today was much better, but it still seems like it would be better to find someone that he can actually get used to."

"I can't find someone else by next week."

"Okay, I understand."

"You clearly don't want to come back."

"I can come back, it's just like I said, it seems like it's not a good fit."

"I hired you for this job. You agreed to this job."

"Okay. I just feel bad that I'm going to have to leave soon. And this isn't my normal rate."

"You agreed to this rate."

"I just thought you were going to keep looking for someone else."

"Why would I do that?"

"I thought you needed to find someone else for the fall anyway."

"No," she said, "I don't. You know what, don't come back."

"I can if you don't find anyone else."

"No, now you lied to me."

"What? I didn't lie about anything."

"Forget it, I'll find someone else."

I glanced over my shoulder to Silas, who was sitting and staring at the floor. I turned around and got my bag and said, "Come on."

We walked toward the front door.

"I'm sorry, I think we had a misunderstanding," I said.

"Please leave," said Susanna.

Silas grabbed his bike and we left.

I got in the car and closed the door. Silas took off his front wheel, put his bike in the trunk, and got in the passenger seat. I backed out of the driveway.

"Oh shit, I think I forgot my phone," he said.

My chest tightened. I took my foot off the gas and looked at him.

"You're going back alone," I said.

"Ha, just kidding." He flashed me his phone.

"Oh my god." I punched him in the arm.

He laughed again.

"Oh my god," I said again. "I can't even believe what happened in there."

"Yeah," said Silas.

"What did happen? Did I just get fired?"

"Yeah, you definitely got fired."

"I didn't lie to her. What would I have even lied to her about?"

"I don't know," said Silas.

"Are you serious? You think I lied to her?"

"No," he said. "Maybe she was just mad that you didn't like her kid."

"I didn't not like her kid," I said. "I just thought that this babysitting job made no sense for anybody. Now I can't even use those pictures. She's not going to sign a release."

"What pictures?"

"I took pictures of the kid and the apartment and stuff. I got this amazing shot of him in the bathtub."

"I'm pretty sure that's illegal."

"No, you can't see anything."

"Oh well," said Silas.

"Never mind," I said. "I don't want to talk about it any-more."

Then I remembered about the money and got it out of my bag. "Count this."

Silas flipped through the bills. "One thirty."

"One thirty?" There was no way that was right. I did the math in my head—it was thirteen and a half hours, so it should have been like a hundred and sixty dollars. "Fuck," I said. "She owes me thirty bucks."

"Oh man," said Silas. "We should get a case of eggs and go back there."

I didn't know if he was joking, or if he would actually do something like that.

"Yeah, that would solve all my problems," I said.

We drove in silence until we got close to his apartment.

"Want to get food?" he said.

"I'm not really hungry," I said.

He ordered Chinese, and when it came I ate all of the scallion pancakes. I sort of wanted Silas to take care of me like he had the night before, but I suspected that my body language was instructing him to steer clear. I wondered what I was going to tell my dad's girlfriend. She probably wasn't going to get me any more babysitting jobs, but I was fine with that. I didn't want her to think it was all my fault, but I wasn't sure whose fault it was. Silas and I watched TV and the more I thought about Timmy and Susanna, the worse I felt. I thought maybe I should apologize either way, even if it was Susanna's fault.

"You bummed about those pictures?" said Silas.

"Yeah, I guess," I said. "And I feel bad about the kid."

"Well," said Silas. "Not all deaf people can be friends."

We kept watching the TV. I couldn't decide whether Silas was actually kind of wise, or a total fucking idiot.

"Okay what about this?" he said a little while later. "My friend's landlord was a total dick and totally dicked him over, so before my friend moved out he superglued all the lightbulbs into the sockets."

"What?"

"Get it? You can get the job back and then you can do that. They'll never know it was you. They won't even know anything happened until the lights start going out, probably in like months, maybe years, and their apartment will be fucked. That's the definition of a perfect crime."

I thought through what that would mean, and imagined Susanna in the dark, trying to change the light, the bulb bursting in her hand.

I got up and went into the bathroom and locked the door. I took a shower and put my underwear and tank top back on and got into bed. When Silas got in, I pretended I was asleep. It was the first night we weren't going to have sex, and I didn't think it would be the last. I let him spoon me, but when I felt his breathing slow and his body get heavy, I climbed over him to the far side of the bed and tried to fall asleep there. I couldn't wait to leave the summer behind.

BARBARA THE SLUT

They called me Barbara the Slut. It started in eleventh grade, and they called me other names, too—*ho, whore, skank, Barbara Lewinsky, sticky-fingers Murphy*—but mostly they called me *slut*.

Maybe I wasn't hard to get, but I did have standards. They were: good teeth and good skin and big hands. And I needed to know that boys were honest, which most of them were. Even the boys who thought they were tricking me were honest in bed. They were honest when they touched me, more honest when I made them come, and the most honest when they made me come.

At the beginning of eleventh grade I slept with a boy

more than once and it made him dishonest. It made him want to do it all the time and it made him do dumb things like have his hands on some other girl's butt all day and then want me to give him a blow job before practice. So now it's one time per boy, and when I run out of boys it'll be time to go to college.

When SLUT got spray-painted in pink letters down the front of my locker at the end of junior year, I had to go to the school therapist to talk about my feelings. I kind of liked the color and I would have been more upset if it had been black or something, but those weren't the feelings the therapist wanted to talk about. She asked me if I thought I was promiscuous and I said no. She said in that case the other kids were just jealous of me being so smart, and I should try to forget about them. She said she didn't need to get in touch with my parents because it was just a misunderstanding. I don't think she was very good at her job. She told me again to try not to think about it. It was easy not to think about girls, but what about boys?

If I heard of a Barbara the Slut, I would think she was nerdy because her name was Barbara, and that she wasn't pretty enough to be popular, so she decided to be a slut instead. I don't know what it takes to be popular, but I don't think being a slut is runner-up to being popular. The truth is that I am nerdy, and maybe it's because my name is Barbara and maybe not. Maybe people who think it's funny to name their kids old-people names like Barbara and George also raise their kids to like numbers and marine mammals more than they like other kids. But the truth is also that I am pretty. My parents are weird but they're good-looking, and my little brother and I got good combinations of their genes. I got my mom's olive skin and dark hair and I got my dad's green eyes. I got my mom's runner's body except with bigger boobs. My teeth are kind of big, but it's not like they're horse teeth or anything. George got the same green eyes but the light skin and the red hair, and we were the same size for a long time, but then all of a sudden he turned into a giant.

George started going to my high school my senior year. He had high-functioning autism and went to special ed, and if he were my kid, I would have sent him to a special school. The kids at Ashwell were really mean. But my parents wouldn't listen. They said they wanted George to have a mainstream experience, like that's a good thing to have. They acted like nothing was wrong with him, or like it was fine that he was autistic. They didn't even notice for the first three years of his life—they noticed that he was slower than me, but they didn't think that meant anything. Sometimes I feel like I should have noticed, but I was three when he was born and six when he was diagnosed.

Now he was doing much better. But I still didn't think he should have to go to my school.

As far as I knew, nobody called George any names on the first day, and nobody called me a slut either. I thought maybe they forgot over the summer. It was good timing because I wasn't going to have sex until my college application was due in November.

I was applying early decision and my GPA was better than perfect and my SAT score was almost perfect, and I was going to write a perfect essay about how math changed my running game. I calculated my average sweat rate and electrolyte loss, converted electrolyte moles to milligrams, and so determined my nutritional needs to eliminate muscle cramping and fatigue. I did all the calculations over the summer and shaved forty seconds per mile off of ten-mile runs. Anyway, I still had to write the essay, and I wanted to take the SATs one more time. I couldn't afford to be distracted by boys.

On the second day of school Nick Caruso asked me if I wanted to go for a drive. Nick was nice enough but one of his teeth was rotten, and also I don't do it in cars, and also I was temporarily abstinent as explained. I told him that I had to take care of my brother, but really George went to the after-school program. More boys asked me that week and I said no, and it turned out that no one had forgotten about the slut thing.

In October I turned seventeen and got called *prude* for the first time, which was funny. I submitted my college application early and my parents took us out for pizza to celebrate. In the parking lot when my mom thought we weren't looking, she stuck her tongue in my dad's ear. Parents of autistic kids are supposed to get divorced, but my parents are still obsessed with each other and it's disgusting. George thought the tongue in the ear was the funniest thing ever and he tried to do it to me and I had to fight him off.

No one had told George about me going to college, so he didn't understand what we were celebrating. My mom explained that I was going to go to a different school, like when we went to different schools last year.

"Except my new school is in New Jersey," I said.

My mom elbowed me.

"Where is New Jersey?" said George.

My parents looked at each other and my mom coughed and my dad adjusted his glasses.

"New Jersey is a town," said my mom, "near Boston." We lived forty minutes north of Boston.

"But you'll pick me up at after-school," George said to me.

"Uh," I said. I was starting to feel guilty that George even had to go to after-school. I had wanted to keep my afternoons free, but now that I was trying not to have sex

I didn't actually have much to do, and I went on long runs and made egg sandwiches while George sat in a classroom and read marine biology books and ate saltines.

"We'll see," my dad told George. My parents were pretty stupid for a math professor and a shrink. Even if George didn't look up New Jersey as soon as we got home, when I got in they were going to have to explain that it was three or four states away, depending on which highways you took, and that I was never going to pick George up at five again.

Three weeks before Thanksgiving, I finally had sex. Jesse Spence showed up at my locker and asked me if I wanted to go to his house after school. I wondered if he hadn't heard that I was on strike, or if he was just really cocky. He said he liked me, which seemed unlikely, but his smile was sweet and he was the senior pitcher for the baseball team and he had huge meaty hands with chewed finger-nails, so I said okay.

Jesse waited for me outside after last period, which was a good sign because some boys didn't. Then they were so mad at themselves for chickening out that they would tell everyone I wanted to sleep with them but they didn't want to sleep with me.

Jesse said, "Hey," and smiled his sweet smile and fol-lowed me to my car.

When we got to his house he put carrot sticks on a plate and said he didn't have any other snacks because his parents were on a diet together. We went up to his room and his bed was made, and I wondered if he always made it or if he was planning on me. I sat on the bed and he sat at his desk.

"How was your summer?" he said.

"It was good," I said. "It was a pretty long time ago. How was yours?"

"It was good," he said.

"You can sit next to me if you want," I said.

He stood up too quickly and his chair rolled back and hit the desk. I laughed and he blushed. I love boys who blush.

He sat next to me and I moved the plate of carrots to the floor. When I sat back up he kissed me and it felt good and warm, like he was still hot from blushing. I kissed him back with tongue because the boys who don't start with tongue are the ones who are good at it.

Jesse kissed me and kissed me and he was going to kiss me all afternoon if I didn't stop him. I pushed him back onto the bed and he looked nervous.

"What?" I said.

"We don't have to do it," he said. "We could just hang out."

"I have to go soon," I said.

"Okay," he said. He let me kiss him and take off his

shirt and pants and boxers until he was naked and I was fully dressed, waiting for him to make a move. Finally he slid his hands under my shirt and they felt like I hoped they would—soft and rough and enough to cover my boobs and a little more. He took off my shirt and bra and I slid out of my pants and underwear. He took a condom out of his drawer and put it on the nightstand but he seemed content just to touch me all over. I felt like I was Cleopatra and he was my boy. It never happens like that. I could have stayed in his bed forever, but it was already after four o'clock. I opened the condom.

"Fuck me," I said.

"Are you sure?" he said.

I laughed and he blushed again.

I left Jesse's house at four fifty and was late to pick up George.

"Barbara, did you hear about the world's loneliest whale?" George said when he got in the car.

"Ha ha," I said. "No, what?"

"This is not a joke about whales, so you shouldn't laugh because it's not a joke. This is a story about a whale with a communication disability."

He buckled his seat belt.

"This whale sings at a fifty-two hertz frequency. The other whales sing at fifteen to twenty-five hertz frequencies. So that means the other whales can't hear her. Only the navy can hear her. The navy is listening to her. They started listening to her in 1989. They know where she is. She doesn't follow the same migration patterns as any of the other whales and the other whales don't know where she is and she doesn't know where they are. The marine biologists think she's a hybrid of two species or the last survivor of an unidentified species. And that's the reason why nobody can hear her."

"Wow," I said.

"Yes," said George.

When we got home George started up the computer to listen to the whale songs and I painted my nails. I replayed the afternoon with Jesse in my head. I wished I could sleep with him again.

"Here is the blue whale song," George said. It sounded like snoring. "Here's the fifty-two hertz whale song," he said. That one sounded like an owl hooting. "Those are sped up so that we can hear them," he said. "Here's what the fifty-two hertz really sounds like. You can't hear it!"

Obviously that one sounded like nothing.

The next time I saw Jesse he asked me if I wanted to hang out that weekend, maybe Sunday morning. But I was not about to let him fuck me on a Sunday morning if he was only offering Sunday because he had better things to do on Friday and Saturday. Sunday morning is the best time of the week to have sex.

I looked for Jesse after that, but I didn't see him at all the next week. Instead I started seeing Roger Vasquez around. Roger was the other pitcher on the baseball team and I had noticed him before. He was tall and dark and he had perfect teeth. He started smiling at me in the hallways and I started smiling back at him. It didn't seem like a good idea to sleep with another boy on the baseball team right away, especially not the junior pitcher. But it was a catch-22 because the baseball team was the best-looking team in school. They weren't stupid like the football team or assholes like the lacrosse team or pretentious like the crew team, and they looked so much stronger than the track team. I liked the swim team, but the boys' and girls' swim teams only slept with each other.

Finally I got tired of all the smiling and decided to talk to Roger. That Friday he walked by while I was waiting outside my brother's classroom to give him his lunch.

"Hey," I said.

"Hi," said Roger.

"What are you up to later?"

"Uh," he said. "Nothing, I'm free."

Then Ms. Danielle opened the door and let George out.

"I forgot my lunch in the car!" said George.

"I know, dummy." I handed him the bag.

Roger looked at the door of the classroom. "Is your brother retarded or something?"

"What?" I said.

"Barbara's brother is not retarded," said George. "But there is a retarded boy I can show you. His name is Christopher."

I didn't look at Roger. "Okay buddy," I told George, "I'll see you at five."

"Okay," he said. He gave me a hug from the side and when he was done I thought he was going to give me a kiss but he stuck his tongue in my ear and I jumped.

"George!" I said.

George smiled.

"Sick," said Roger.

"Why are you still here?" I said to him. He looked nervous. "Go away." I knocked on the door and Ms. Danielle let George back in.

"I'm serious," I said. "Go away. I wouldn't sleep with you in a million years."

"Whatever," Roger said, and started walking away. "Slut."

"Fuck you," I said. "What's wrong with you?"

Roger told everyone that he fucked me, and he started calling me a slut whenever he saw me. Like, "Hey, slut," or

"What up, slut?" Then the rest of the baseball team started saying hi to me and calling me *slut*. And then some girls who liked Roger started calling me a slut, but not saying hi. When I finally ran into Jesse again he didn't look at me and I knew he was mad. I wanted to tell him that I didn't sleep with Roger but I knew he wouldn't believe me.

I tried to forget about Roger and Jesse when we left for Turks and Caicos for Thanksgiving, but on the plane George said that he saw my boyfriend, and my mom said, "Boyfriend?" and George said, "I said Christopher is the retarded one," and my mom said, "What is he talking about?" and I said, "I have no idea." For the rest of the week whenever I looked at George, I imagined Roger calling him a retard and I felt dizzy.

Roger did not shut up about me being a slut. I started counting how many times he called me one, and by December 15 it was fifty-four. That was it for the day because at eleven thirty I left school with a note from my mom. At home I logged in to my application account, and from eleven fifty to eleven fifty-nine I ran up and down the stairs. At twelve I got into Princeton.

I called my mom and she started screaming, "I knew it! I knew it!" before I could even tell her. She must have pushed her twelve o'clock back, and I thought about the patient sitting in the waiting room and listening to her yell, "I knew it!"

Then I called my dad and he said, "Congratulations, angel, that's very exciting," which is exactly what I knew he was going to say. Everything went exactly the way I thought it was going to go. I had tried to pretend that I didn't know I was going to get in, but like I said, the odds were pretty good. In addition to my grades and test scores, it just so happened that both of my parents went to Princeton. When I was in the process of applying, the admissions counselor at school told me that one other student from Ashwell had been admitted to Princeton, three years ago, and she wasn't a legacy but she was black. What she actually said was, "She had a diverse background," which didn't make any sense.

I spent the afternoon looking at the course catalog and making a list of classes I wanted to take. When I was done with that I downloaded a picture of four girls on the Princeton cross-country team and Photoshopped my face onto the one who looked the most like me. The girls had their arms around each other like older, sweatier versions of the girls in my elementary school yearbooks. It took me an hour but I did a good job. I printed it out on photo paper and put it in my mirror with the pictures from Turks and Caicos and a math team picture from when we won the New England Meet junior year.

I went for a run and let my parents pick George up from after-school. When they got home with him we went out to dinner at the Indian place, and when we got back my mom took a new Princeton sweatshirt out of her bedroom and a cake box out of the cabinet over the stove. My dad got a bottle of champagne out of the fridge and poured glasses for the three of us and a glass of milk for my brother.

"To Barbara the mathematician," said my dad and raised his glass.

"To Barbara, my college girl," said my mom.

"To Barbara the Slud," George said and thumped me on the back.

I froze.

My dad put his glass down on the counter too hard.

"What?" said my mom. "What did you say, George?"

George looked at her and at my dad. He looked at me and then looked away and drank all of his milk.

"George, that sounded like a bad word," said my mom. "Did you mean to say a bad word?"

"No!" said George. "It's not a bad word."

"Where did you hear that?" said my dad.

"It's not a bad word," said George.

"I'm sure that's not what he meant," I said. "I'm sure it's not what it sounds like."

My mom looked at me and started cutting the cake, a coconut cake like the one from Connie's on Cape Cod. Everyone was silent. I ate two big pieces and tried to calm down.

"Here come the freshman fifteen," my dad said when I finished.

"Neil!" said my mom.

"Sorry." My dad winked at me. "But keep up the running."

My mom rolled her eyes.

When we were done eating I went to my room. My stomach churned. I e-mailed my guidance counselor about Princeton and finally my mom knocked, even though the door was open.

"Hi honey," she said. "Is there anything you want to talk about?"

"No," I said.

"Is everything okay at school?"

"Yes," I said.

"Well, when George . . ." she said.

"George is retarded," I said.

My mom studied me. "I can tell you don't want to talk about this, Barbara. But calling your brother retarded is not the way to get out of it." My mom's therapy voice makes me want to crawl back into her womb where I can't hear her.

"Everything is fine," I said. "I don't know where George got that. But everything is fine."

"Okay," she said. "I need you to tell me if I should worry."

"Okay," I said. "I will."

. . .

The next day was Friday and I tried to forget about my mom and dad and George. I wore my new sweatshirt to show everyone at school that I was out of there. When I got to homeroom Ms. Constantino congratulated me. Then the bell rang and she made announcements about next week's finals that nobody listened to.

"And we have our second early-admission notification," she said. "Barbara Murphy was admitted to Princeton University." Somebody booed. Ms. Constantino looked up and frowned. "Barbara is the second student from Ashwell ever to be accepted to Princeton, so congratulations, Barbara."

"Slut," said a girl in the back of the room.

"Kelsey! See me after the bell!" said Ms. Constantino. She looked at the paper in her hand and read, "The shoe drive will end next Friday, December twenty-third. Please bring in new or gently worn shoes and deposit them in the boxes by the main office and the gym entrance."

I tried to hurry out of the classroom when the bell rang.

"Who do you know in admissions?" said Joanna De-Marco. She stuck her tongue in her cheek and pumped her hand like she was giving a blow job.

At lunch I went to the cafeteria to get chocolate milk and somebody yelled "whore" so I went to eat in my car. When

I finished my coconut cake I felt better and decided to spend the rest of the period reading in the library instead of listening to "Tiny Dancer" on repeat.

Roger Vasquez was sitting outside the library with Lacey Hill on his lap and Melissa Knight next to him.

"Hey Princeton slut," Roger said when he saw me.

Lacey turned around. "Barbara the Slut," she said and stood up.

I walked into the library and headed for the desk across the room. The librarian had headphones on and was looking at her computer.

"Not so fast," said Melissa. She grabbed my bag and it slid off my shoulder and onto the floor.

Lacey got in front of me. "You think you're so great."

"No," I said.

She pushed my chest and I had to take a step back. I felt like I was going to pee. I tried to get out from between her and Melissa. Roger was standing in the door of the library.

"What's the re-tard going to do when you're being a sl-ut at P-rince-ton?" said Melissa.

I thought Lacey was going to push me again, but she grabbed my boobs and dug her fingers in. I took her wrists and tried to get her to let go. I wanted to say something but no words would come out. Finally I yelled, "Help!"

The librarian took off her headphones but didn't stand up. "What is going on here?" she said.

"Nothing." Lacey smiled at her. She patted me on the head. "See you later, Barbara."

"I need help." I grabbed my bag and ran toward the desk.

"Pussy," said Melissa.

When I got to the desk the librarian looked at me and I turned to see the three of them leaving.

"It's okay," I said. "I'll look for the book myself. If I can't find it I'll come back."

"Okay," said the librarian and put her headphones back on.

I went back to the stacks but two kids were making out on a step stool. No one was in the library classroom so I went in and lay down under one of the tables and looked at the wads of gum. I couldn't stop shaking.

When the bell rang I got out from under the table and took my sweatshirt off. I looked into my shirt and my boobs looked okay. I put the sweatshirt in my locker and went to chemistry and then AP Calculus. Mr. Monahan was really excited about Princeton and gave me a hug. It made my throat tighten and I had to pull away from him. After calculus I got my bag and my sweatshirt out of my locker and went outside.

In the parking lot I heard a car accelerating behind me and something heavy hit me in the back of the leg. A Diet Coke can rolled away. The car sped past me and a girl leaned out the window and yelled, "Go kill yourself, slut!"

It was Amber Battaglia, and the car looked like the CR-V that Jesse Spence got over Thanksgiving, and as it drove away I tried to remember if Amber and Jesse knew each other or not.

My leg was throbbing when I got to my car. I got in, locked the doors, and tried to get the key into the ignition but it took me a minute. I drove home slowly because I was worried that if I drove fast I would get in an accident. I thought about what it would feel like right before, and how quickly it could be over. No one would put a cross with flowers next to the accident site because my parents would think it was trashy, and no one at school would do that for me. George would do it if he knew I wanted him to, but he wouldn't know I wanted him to.

When I got home I didn't want to go inside, so I started the car again and drove back to school. My heart was still beating too fast when I got there. I felt panicked that they weren't going to let George go because it wasn't five o'clock, but they did because I told them that our pretend dog Lemma was dying and George had to come say good-bye. George looked happy to see me until I pulled him into a hug and whispered, "Start crying right now."

Since George was the smartest kid in the world, he started sniffling.

When we got outside he said, "Can I watch a movie with you tonight?"

I thought about taking him to a movie right then but I

was scared to be in a dark theater. "Yeah," I said. "We can watch a movie tonight."

"Where are we going?" said George. "This isn't the way to go home."

I had been planning on driving around, but he wasn't going to go for it.

"We're going to get ice cream," I said. I turned around again.

"Ice cream is for the summer not the winter," George said.

When we got to Friendly's he reconsidered and ordered a Jim Dandy with scoops of strawberry, chocolate, black raspberry, mint chocolate chip, and Vienna mocha chunk. I didn't have a good feeling about it, but when it came in a huge wineglass-shaped dish, it was the perfect sundae. We ate half of it and then I sent George out to the car with my keys and he came back with his backpack and my book for current events. I read and George did his sudoku book, and when the sundae melted we took sips of it.

We left Friendly's at five and we got home at the same time as our mom. I didn't think my parents would be there because it was their date night, but my mom said they were going to a nice restaurant and she wanted to put on a dress.

I went to my room to put my stuff down and got into bed. I felt sick from the sundae. My mom came in to tell me she was leaving. She was wearing a black sweater dress and a turquoise necklace and I wondered if I was going to be beautiful like her when I was somebody's mom.

"Are you okay, honey?" she said.

"Yeah," I said. "I ate too much ice cream."

"It was sweet of you to pick George up early," she said. "Were your teachers excited?"

"Yeah," I said.

My mom kissed my hair and left.

Now that I was in bed and I wasn't shaking and my heart wasn't beating in my ears and I wasn't distracted by George, I was mad. Roger Fucking Vasquez, I wanted to kill him. I got out of bed and looked him up in the phone book.

I dialed his number and got his mom.

"Hi, may I please speak to Roger?" I said.

"Sure, just a minute," she said. I heard the phone hit a table or something, and she called, "Roger, it's a girl!"

"Hello?" said Roger.

"It's Barbara," I said. "If you ever call me a slut again, I'll tell everyone at school you couldn't keep it up when we fucked. Okay?"

He didn't say anything but I could hear him breathing.

"And I heard you need a baseball scholarship because you're so dumb, and you probably wouldn't want me to call your recruiters and tell them that you do steroids and you're suffering from testicular atrophy."

More breathing.

"I'm sure you don't know what that means, but it's when your balls deflate."

I hung up because it didn't seem like Roger had anything to add. I didn't think threatening Roger was going to make things better with Lacey or Melissa or anyone else, but I did think he was going to make the right choice.

Next I looked up Jesse Spence's address and went downstairs.

"We have to go out for a minute," I told George.

"You said we were going to watch a movie."

"We will when we get back."

In the car George announced that it had been one minute.

"A minute means a lot of minutes," I said.

"No it doesn't, it means one minute."

"Okay, well, we're going out for a lot of minutes." I pushed the tape into the deck and "Tiny Dancer" came back on. George sang along, and I felt my forehead relax. When we got to Jesse's house the CR-V was in the driveway. I told George to stay in the car.

"Have a good time," he said.

I squeezed his knee. I didn't know what I was going to do without that kid.

I got out and walked across the lawn. It was a cold, clear night.

I knocked. I hoped Jesse's parents were out dieting or something.

Jesse answered the door after a minute and looked surprised.

"Listen, I'm sorry about Amber throwing that soda at you," he said, almost whispering. "I didn't know she was going to do that."

"Uh," I said.

"Okay," he said, "have a good night."

I put my hand on the door. He looked up the stairs behind him, and then back at me.

"Do you want to hang out again sometime?" I said. "I'll break the rule."

"What rule?" he said.

"I don't sleep with people more than once," I said.

"Jesus, Barbara." He stared at me and I stared back. "Do you ever wonder why people call you names?"

"No," I said. I started to shiver.

"I don't want to sleep with you again," he said. "I wish I knew about the rule before."

"Well," I said. "Sorry." I heard a door open upstairs.

"You should go," he said. "I hope your leg is okay."

"I didn't sleep with Roger," I said.

He opened his mouth but nothing came out.

I walked back across the lawn.

By the time I got to the car I was really cold.

George took my hand and rubbed it between his.

"Is that your friend?" he said.

"No," I said.

"He's not my friend either," he said.

I drove. George kept my hand and rubbed it until my skin burned.

ACKNOWLEDGMENTS

P.E. (a.k.a. Alicia Erian)—thank you for telling me I could do it, thank you for teaching me how, and thank you for a decade of advice, encouragement, and love. Colum McCann—thank you for being my champion and for pushing me further than I thought I could go. Peter Carey—thank you for making magic at Hunter and for saying that sometimes it's enough to be funny. Nathan Englander—thank you for being my mentor and my friend, thank you for being there for me at every stage of this book, and thank you for teaching me so much of what I know about words, sentences, and stories.

Phil Klay—thank you for making me write this book (I should have known it would take a Marine), and for reading every word one million times. Jessica Ruth Lacher—thank you for also reading every word one million times, and for all the tough love.

To my agent, Duvall Osteen—thank you for believing in me, thank you for guiding me, thank you for doing all the hard parts. You're a real badass, and I'm grateful and honored to have you as my agent and my friend.

To my magical editor, Becky Saletan—thank you for seeing what I hoped you would see in this book, and for editing it so organically and so brilliantly.

To the team at Riverhead—Geoff Kloske, Claire McGinnis, Glory Anne Plata, Katie Freeman, Jynne Martin, Michelle Koufopoulos, Deborah Weiss Geline, Meighan Cavanaugh, and Rachel Willey—thank you for everything. I'm so lucky to work with you.

Casey Leon—thank you for reading and laughing. Kate Sarrantonio—thank you for your careful and conscious reads.

Thank you to all the writers, teachers, friends, and other champions who inspired me, taught me, read for me, and supported me before, during, and after this book—there are too many of you to name but you know who you are.

To my family—you're the most important characters in my life, even though you aren't characters in this book (I hope you're grateful for that). Thank you for always listening to my stories, even when they were super fucking boring. Thank you for your unlimited love and support.

And even though Honey is dead and Rhoda and Tallulah can't read, thank you to my three dogs for keeping me company while I worked, for inspiring me, for making me laugh, and for rescuing me from the loneliness of being human.